FORTY LOVE

FORTY LOVE

JACK SHOLL

authorHOUSE®

AuthorHouse™ LLC
1663 Liberty Drive
Bloomington, IN 47403
www.authorhouse.com
Phone: 1-800-839-8640

This is a work of fiction. Names, characters, places and
incidents either are the product of the author's imagination
or are used fictitiously, and any resemblance to actual
persons, living or dead, businesses, companies, products,
events or locales is entirely concidental.

Published by AuthorHouse   01/28/2014

ISBN: 978-1-4918-3859-4 (sc)
ISBN: 978-1-4918-3920-1 (hc)
ISBN: 978-1-4918-3651-4 (e)

Library of Congress Control Number: 2013921170

Any people depicted in stock imagery provided by Thinkstock
are models, and such images are being used for illustrative
purposes only. Certain stock imagery © Thinkstock.

This book is printed on acid-free paper.

FADE IN:

INT. BENNINGTON HOUSE—DAY

A collection of photos and memorabilia is on the mantle of a fireplace and then an adjoining bookshelf. CAMERA PANS a framed photo of a man in his 30s in tennis shorts and tennis sweater holding a tennis racquet, a framed photo of the same man with the legendary tennis player Arthur Ashe with an inscription "To Don, one of the greatest— Arthur", a commemorative medal with an engraved profile of a tennis player, victory ribbons, plaques, trophies, a framed photo of tennis match in a stadium between two men, the man in combat pilot attire in front of a U.S. Air Force jet, and a framed photo of the man in tennis attire with a little girl.

The THUNK THUNK THUNK of a tennis ball hitting an outside garage door.

EXT. BENNINGTON HOUSE-DRIVEWAY-DAY

JANE BENNINGTON, a pert blonde high school senior who is the prototypical all-American girl next door, actively dashes about with a tennis racquet as she hits a tennis ball against the garage door. She is in shorts and a T-shirt. She has a snub nose and perfect white teeth and medium length hair. The Bennington house is in a middle-class residential community in southern California.

INT./EXT. CAR—DAY

MRS. BENNINGTON P.O.V.—

CAMERA PANS houses along street and then driveway as LOUISE BENNINGTON watches Jane hitting the ball. She BEEPS the car horn and pulls into the driveway. Louise Bennington is in her mid-forties. She is wearing a Seven-Eleven convenience store uniform and has just returned home from work. She exits the car and embraces Jane.

> LOUISE
> Hi, honey. I'm going to throw together some dinner. Come on in a few minutes. Don't you think that's enough for one day?

> JANE
> OK, Mom. But, gosh, how'm I going to get better if I don't practice?

Louise walks up the steps of the small porch.

> LOUISE
> OK. Just a little longer but you've got to come in for dinner.

INT. BENNINGTON HOUSE—DAY

LIVING ROOM

Louise walks though the living room and into the kitchen. She takes three TV dinners from the refrigerator and puts them in the oven. She then walks back to the living room and calls up the stairs.

                    LOUISE
     Tad! Come on down. Dinner will be
     ready shortly.

TAD'S BEDROOM

Tad, Jane's 14 year-old younger brother, is
sitting in front of a computer at a desk
doing his homework.

                    LOUISE (V.O.)
     Dinner, Tad. Come down in a few
     minutes.

KITCHEN

Louise and Tad are at the table with the
TV dinners in front of them. Jane very
energetically comes through the door, puts
her tennis racquet against the wall and plops
into her seat.

                    JANE
     How was your day, Mom?

                    LOUISE
     Oh, you know how I hate to complain.
     But terrible. Just terrible. I have
     such a splitting headache. People
     are so inconsiderate.

                    JANE
     Mom, Denise invited me over to play
     tennis at her club Saturday. Would
     it be okay if I go?

LOUISE

I thought you were going to help me
clean house this weekend.

JANE

Oh, Mom, you know I'll help you, and
I promise I won't be gone all day. I
need to keep up my game and it's so
hard to get court time over at the
park on weekends.

LOUISE

Oh, I suppose. I'm sorry, it's
just that since your dad died
things haven't been so well. I wish
he'd never decided to stay in the
Reserves. It's been so hard to get
along, and all. I know you love
tennis and you're so good, just like
your dad. If he were still here, we
could join Marbella and you could
play all you want.

JANE

Thanks, Mom.

LOUISE

That Marbella Club, though, Jane.
Don't get any fancy ideas. We just
don't have the money.

JANE

Yes, Mom. I know.

EXT. LAGUNA HILLS HIGH SCHOOL—DAY

TENNIS COURTS

Jane and a GIRL are hitting a ball back
and forth. Jane slams the ball across the
court just inside the baseline beyond her
opponent's reach.

BENCH—LATER

> DENISE
> Jeez, you made short work of her. I
> wish I could play like you. The team
> would be nothing without you. Are
> you still thinking about going pro?

> JANE
> Oh, I don't know. I have to think
> about college still.

> DENISE
> Oh, yeah. Veterinarian school?

> JANE
> Yeah, if I can get in. Maybe I can
> play for Cal State. But going pro?
> I mean that's a dream. I don't even
> know how I'd go about it.

> DENISE
> Hey, look, there's Roger.

TENNIS COURT STANDS

A young man, ROGER, Jane's boyfriend waves
and SMILES.

Jane SMILES and waives.

> DENISE
> He's so adorable!

                    JANE
      Yeah, isn't he?

                   DENISE
      Are you going out tonight?

                    JANE
      No, I've got to help my Mom.

                   DENISE
      You are coming to the club with me
      tomorrow?

                    JANE
      Oh, yeah. I wouldn't miss that for
      the world.

The COACH walks by.

                   COACH
      Good game, Jane. Real good game.

                    JANE
      Thanks coach.

Turns to Denise.

                 JANE (contd.)
      See you tomorrow. Gotta go.

Jane goes running off to join Roger who has
come down the stands and is walking toward
her.

EXT. MARBELLA COUNTY CLUB—DAY

SIGN—"MARBELLA COUNTY CLUB. PRIVATE. MEMBERS
AND GUESTS ONLY."

Jane and Denise are walking out of the door
of the clubhouse and the CAMERA DOLLIES as
they walk along the elevated walkway by the
courts. Denise is wearing a tennis skirt and
sweater. Jane is wearing plaid shorts and a
T-shirt.

>   JANE
> Oh, it's so wonderful here. I wish
> we could afford to belong. I'd be
> here all the time. I'd never get off
> the court.
> (Pause)
> Oh, isn't that Veronica Tyson?

JANE'S P.O.V.—LOOKING AT NEIGHBORING TENNIS
COURT

LANCE DRAKE, a fit man of about 40 years old,
is serving balls to VERONICA TYSON. She
is powerfully smashing balls back to him.
Veronica's long black hair is pushed back
under a red headband.

>   JANE
> She's so good. Now there's someone
> who should go pro.

>   DENISE
> Well, that's just because she takes
> lessons from Lance Drake. He's the
> club pro. That's him there. She also
> was at John Boloti's Tennis Camp
> in Florida. You're so much better
> than she is, and you know it. You've
> beaten her every time we've played
> Matre Dei Prep. Besides, she's such
> a bitch.

> JANE
> Why do you say that?

> DENISE
> She's just awful. She's so stuck up.
> Because of all the money her parents
> have. She's got everything.

Jane and Denise walk into court and take out
their racquets at the bench.

> JANE
> Lance Drake was on the WTA tour.
> How long's he been the pro here? I
> used to follow him when my Dad was
> playing.

> DENISE
> Oh, I guess for a couple of years
> now. He was doing all those
> commercials and stuff, and I guess
> he got more interested in that than
> playing all the time. At least, he
> made more money.

> JANE
> Come on, let's play.

Jane serves.

Jane and Denise hit the ball back and forth.

Jane and Denise finish the game and exit the
court. Outside in the walkway is Lance.

LANCE
Hi, Denise. See you're still hitting
your backhand like I showed you.
Who's your friend, here? New member?

DENISE
This is Jane Bennington, she's a
friend of mine from school. We're on
the tennis team together. Jane, this
is Lance Drake, our tennis pro.

JANE
I remember you when you played
Forest Lawn. Glad to meet you, sir.

LANCE
That was a while ago. Always got
to make room for new talent. I was
watching you play. You've got great
form, a natural ability. Just like
Navatrilova in her younger days,
when she was just starting out.

JANE
You're just being too nice. But
anything I know about tennis I must
have inherited it from my father.
Don Bennington. Do you remember him
at all?

LANCE
Don Bennington! Why sure. So you're
Don Bennington's daughter.

JANE
Yup!

> LANCE
Say, that's really something! How
about if you and I hit around a bit
sometime?

> JANE
Oh, I'd like that. But we're not
members. I'm just Denise's guest. I
play over at school or on the courts
at the playground.

> LANCE
Oh, I'm sure we can arrange
something here. The pro gets to have
a guest or two. Or maybe Denise
would be nice enough to invite you
back one of these days.

> DENISE
Sure.

Veronica walks up. She is tallish, sleek and
tanned bronze. She is in very stylish tennis
attire, wearing a gold tennis bracelet and
a gold tennis necklace. Her black hair is
gleaming and lustrous, her sleek young tanned
legs coming out from a thigh-high white
tennis skirt.

> VERONICA
Lance, I've been looking all over
for you. Let's go to the clubhouse
and get a soda. Let's go over my
game. These two amateurs will have
to do for themselves.

> LANCE
Denise, Jane, see you later.

INT. BENNINGTON HOUSE—NIGHT

Jane, Lance and Louise are sitting around the
kitchen table.

                    LANCE
     Louise, I think Jane's got the gift.
     It's in her blood.

                    LOUISE
     Tennis's been Jane's whole life. I
     remember even when she was small,
     Don used to tie a string between two
     chairs in the living room and they'd
     use their hands and bat a tennis
     ball back and forth between them.
     And she's always admired her father
     so. She used to watch every game of
     his she could.

                    LANCE
     I know he'd be so proud. She's got
     the making of a champ, all right.
     Steffi Graf, Martina Hingis, Arantxa
     Sanchez-Vicorio—all started early. I
     know. I've seen it all. Believe me.

                    LOUISE
     But becoming a pro, it takes so much
     time. So much pressure. And then
     there's school, Don always resisted
     it so much. To take a chance to
     leave school and give up the chance
     for a real career—Jane wants to be a
     veterinarian—I really don't know.

                    LANCE
I know things haven't been the same
since Don's death but a couple of
good years on the pro tour and Jane
and you'd be made for life. Believe
me. And I'd say that to someone with
less talent.

                    JANE
Mom, what do you think?

                    LOUISE
Well, I just don't know. I admit it
would be great not to have to worry
about where our next dollar's coming
from, but I just don't want Jane to
throw her life away. She's such a
good student. And I know she could
get a scholarship to veterinarian
school.

                    LANCE
Look, how about this? We enter her
in some tournaments, just to start.
We see how it goes. If I'm right, we
can decide as we go along.

                    LOUISE
That seems reasonable.

                    LANCE
There's the California Junior Open a
month from now. Let's enter Jane and
give her a chance to show her stuff.

                    LOUISE
Jane?

JANE
Wow, Mom, that'd be great!

EXT. LAGUNA HILLS HIGH SCHOOL—DAY

Jane and Roger are walking hand in hand on
the campus between classes.

JANE
And so I'll be going next week to
Indian Wells, for the whole weekend.

ROGER
I wish I could go and see you play.
You'll do terrific.

JANE
Are you sure you can't go?

ROGER
Gosh, Jane. We've got finals coming
up. I just have to get a good grade
in calculus. It's my hardest class,
and if I don't get an A, I won't be
able to have the grades for college.

JANE
Yeah, I know. I've got to study
extra hard with all this practice
and everything. I don't know if it's
worth it. I guess so.

ROGER
You'll do fine. You've got
everything. Looks, brains and
talent. What more could you want?
What more could anybody want?

                         JANE
     A kiss.

He kisses her.

EXT. INDIAN WELLS HYATT—GRAND CHAMPIONS
RESORT—DAY

"CALIFORNIA   JUNIOR   DIVISION,   ALL-STATE
DIVISION, ALL-STATE TENNIS CLASSIC"

Crowd in stands.

Lance and Louise in seats.

Jane and Russell in court.

Jane, in short thigh-high tennis skirt and
nylon jersey, bounces the ball three times.
She raises her racquet high.

Across   the   court   is   MARY   RUSSELL,   a
curvaceous young cutie with a shock of blond
hair tumbling from her headband.

Jane brings the racquet down in a swift arch.

The ball whizzes past Mary. She aces her.

Jane walks to the other side of the court.
She is all intensity. She bounces the ball
several times. Mary bounces up and down in
place, on one foot and then the other. She is
all readiness.

Jane serves.

Mary's racquet is poised in mid-swing. She deftly returns the ball.

They hit the ball back and forth. Jane takes the point by delivering a solid volley across the court and past Mary.

INSET
- - - - - - - - - -
SCOREBOARD

	Game	Set 1
Bennington	30	6
Russell	15	3
- - - - - - - - - -

Jane serves.

They rally. Jane rockets a forehand winner past a charging Mary.

INSET
- - - - - - - -
SCOREBOARD

	Game
Bennington	40
Russell	15
- - - - - - - -

CLOSE UP—LANCE AND LOUISE

CLOSE UP—JANE

Jane serves.

They rally. Mary traps Jane behind the base line. Jane returns and Mary delivers a drop shot out of Jane's reach.

INSET
- - - - - - - -
SCOREBOARD

	Game
Bennington	15
Russell	15

- - - - - - - -

Mary serves.

They volley. Mary takes the next four games. In the fifth game, Jane smashes a forehand and Mary hits it into the net.

INSET
- - - - - - - - - - - - - - - - - -
SCOREBOARD

	Game	Set 1	Set 2	Set 3
Bennington	40	6	2	5
Russell	30	3	6	4

- - - - - - - - - - - - - - - - - -

Jane perspires heavily.

Break and match point. Jane smashes a wicked backhand shot across the net. It whizzes past Russell at break point. Jane wins.

INSET
- - - - - - - - - - - - - - -
SCOREBOARD

	Set 1	Set 2	Set 3
Bennington	6	2	6
Russell	3	6	4

- - - - - - - - - - - - - - -

STANDS

Lance and Louise cheer.

INT. RESTAURANT—NIGHT

Jane, Louise and Lance are at a table in an expensive, upscale restaurant celebrating the day's victory. The WAITRESS takes their order.

>   LOUISE
> Oh, I don't know what to have. Maybe just some spaghetti.

>   LANCE
> Oh no you don't. Here your daughter's just beaten one of the top seeds in California high school competition, and you want spaghetti. No way. You're going to have lobster, and, we're going to have some wine, too, to celebrate.

>   LOUISE
> But no wine.
>   LANCE
> That's true, little lady. You're in training, so a soda for you. And a bottle of Merlot for us.
> But Jane, no spaghetti for you, either. How about a nice filet mignon? Gotta keep the stamina up. There's a Junior League competition in Le Habra next month. It's a prize competition. The winner takes five thousand dollars. I think we ought to enter Jane.

> LOUISE
> This is all going a little too fast
> for me, Lance.

> LANCE
> That's the way the world is. Been
> there, done that. Believe me, now's
> the time. All the really tennis
> greats have started young. It just
> takes commitment.

> LOUISE
> Jane?

> JANE
> Gosh, mom, I don't know. I really
> love to play tennis. And, Dad,
> wouldn't he be so proud?

EXT. BENNINGTON HOUSE—NIGHT

Lance waves from the car window as Jane and
Louise walk in the nighttime air up the
driveway to the front door.

> LOUISE
> What a wonderful day! My goodness,
> I can't remember when I've had
> lobster, not even to think about
> wine in a restaurant.

> JANE
> I'm glad to see you so happy, Mom.

> LOUISE
> Oh, well. Tomorrow's another day.
> Donuts and coffee. And donuts
> and coffee and cigarettes. And

newspapers, donuts and coffee and
cigarettes.

                    JANE
     I know, Mom.

EXT. LA HABRA COUNTRY CLUB—DAY

CLUB HOUSE SIGN—"CALIFORNIA OPEN"

FULL SHOT—CROWD IN STANDS

MEDIUM SHOT—LANCE AND LOUISE IN SEATS

INSET
- - - - - - - - - - - - - - - - - -
SCOREBOARD
          Game Set 1 Set 2 Set 3
Bennington
Campbell
- - - - - - - - - - - - - - - - - -

Jane is jumping up and down in place, on one
foot and then the other, her skirt bouncing
up and down. She is alert and tense.

On the other side of the court is KINGSLEY
CAMPBELL, a brown-haired gamin. Kingsley
serves.

INSET
- - - - - - - - - - - - - - -
 SCOREBOARD
             Game Set 1
Bennington   30   6
Campbell   30   4
- - - - - - - - - - - - - -

Kingsley makes a forehand error.

She slams an overhead into the net at 15-15. The game goes to break point.

Jane serves a cascade of puffballs. This goads Campbell into a swinging backhand volley, making errors on the fourth point.

Campbell then creeps back to knot a tie.

She slams a forehand into the net, and then there is a lengthy rally at set point, where she slams another forehand into the net and gives the second set to Jane.

INSET
- - - - - - - - - - - - - - -
SCOREBOARD

	Game	Set 1	Set 2
Bennington	40	4	6
Campbell	30	6	4

- - - - - - - - - - - - - - -

CAMERA is behind Campbell as she delivers a hard serve to Jane, who deftly returns the ball.

They hit the ball back and forth as Jane takes the point by delivering a solid across the court shot.

                                        FADE TO:

INSET
- - - - - - - - - - - - - - - - -
SCOREBOARD

	Game	Set 1	Set 2	Set 3
Bennington	30	4	6	3
Campbell	30	6	4	2
- - - - - - - - - - - - - - - - -

In the third set, fifth game, Jane hits some defensive lobs and Campbell hits an overhead into the net.

Break point and match point: they rally. Campbell swings backhand and the ball goes wide of court. Jane wins the match.

INSET
- - - - - - - - - - - - - - - - -
SCOREBOARD

	Game	Set 1	Set 2	Set 3
Bennington	6	4	6	6
Campbell	4	6	3	4
- - - - - - - - - - - - - - - - -

Jane punches the air with a closed fist, signaling victory.

In the stands, Louise and Lance stand up and cheer.

Jane is beaming.

INT. BENNINGTON HOUSE—DAY

Tad is in the living room foyer. He sees a man is standing in the open doorway. He calls for Louise.

> TAD
> Hey Mom, there's some man here.

> LOUISE
> What's he want?

> TAD
> I don't know. Something about Sis.

> LOUISE
> OK, just a minute.

Louise enters the living room in a house frock, slippers and curlers.

> LOUISE
> Jane's at the library studying. Can I help you?

> SPORTS REP
> Mrs. Bennington, I'm from the Wilson Sporting Goods Company and I'd like to give Jane these six Wilson racquets, covers and a year's supply of Wilson tennis balls. No strings attached, to pardon the phrase.

> LOUISE
> Well, I'll be.

Tad takes a can of balls, dumps them on the floor and watches them bounce.

> TAD
> Wow!

EXT. COLUMBUS, OHIO—HOLIDAY INN—DAY

INT. HOTEL ROOM—NIGHT

Jane is sitting on the bed with her schoolbooks open in front of her. She is on the phone with Roger.

> JANE
> And I won first place. I can't believe it. Mom's all excited, too. When we get home, we're going to buy a new car.

INT. ROGER'S HOUSE BEDROOM—SIMULTANEOUS

> ROGER
> So, when do you think you'll be home, Jane? The Junior Prom is this weekend, remember? You said you'd go with me.

> JANE
> Oh, yeah. That's right. I've been so busy, I forgot. I'm not sure. We won't be home until tomorrow night, and then I've got all this homework to catch up on. It's great that Mrs. Smith said I could take time off to play and everything, but I've got so much work to do. And then Lance wants me to practice both days over the weekend. I'll let you know.

> ROGER
> But I need to know now if you're not going. I rented a Tux and everything.

                    JANE
    Roger, you're so wonderful but I
    just don't think so. I'll ask Mom
    when she gets in. I'll talk to you
    later.

Louise and Lance enter the door of the room.
Lance waves to Jane from the doorway.

                    LANCE
    How're the studies?

                    JANE
    Oh, OK. I'm done with math. Now I've
    got to start history.

                    LANCE
    Don't stay up too late. It'll ruin
    your concentration on the court.

Turns to Louise.

                    LANCE (contd.)
    Good night, Louise. See you in the
    morning.

Lance leaves and Louise admires herself in
the mirror over the bureau. She combs her
hair. Jane, sitting on the bed, is reflected
in the mirror.

                    JANE
    You look great, Mom. Where did you
    go?

                    LOUISE
    We just had drinks at the bar here
    in the hotel.

JANE
What do you think of Lance?

LOUISE
Oh, he's very nice. He really knows
tennis. He's got so much faith in
you. And so many good ideas, we're
really lucky he's taken interest in
you, Jane.
(Pause)
Did Tad call?

JANE
Yeah, he's OK. He's going over to
Fred's after school and then Aunt
Sally will pick 'em up.

LOUISE
Oh, that's good.

JANE
And I talked to Roger. I forgot, the
Prom's this weekend. I told him I
wasn't sure I could go now, with all
this homework and practice.

LOUISE
Oh, my goodness, yes. I know how
much you wanted to go. But you can't
get behind in your schoolwork and
your practice. And, also, Lance said
he wanted to go over some things
Saturday night after practice. He's
got a schedule he wants to go over.

JANE
OK, Mom, I guess all of this is as
important to you and Tad and, Dad,

too, as to me. I'll just tell Roger
I can't.

EXT. LAGUNA HILLS HIGH SCHOOL—DAY

DOOR—"DEAN'S OFFICE" IN GOLD LETTERING.

INT. DEAN'S OFFICE—DAY

Jane and Louise are sitting in chairs in
front of the desk in her office. DEAN ABIGAIL
MOFFET is reviewing a manila file folder that
sits in front of her on the desk.

> DEAN
> Well, Jane, you've certainly been
> applying yourself. I wish I could
> say that for many of our students
> who aren't even doing half the
> things you're doing. All A's. It's
> pretty hard to argue with that.

> LOUISE
> So, you think that Jane could take
> the rest of the year off?

> DEAN
> Well, she's certainly done well
> so far. And if she just keeps up
> the same, then academically, there
> shouldn't be a problem. Of course,
> she'll have to periodically take
> tests, but we could arrange that.
> The question is, though, whether you
> want to do this, Jane. It's a big
> step. You won't have any of your
> friends or schoolmates about. And
> there are a lot of school social

activities you'll miss out on. And while we have every expectation that everything will work out, you don't want to jeopardize going to college. I mean the time you spend practicing and on the road is time you could be doing an internship at an animal hospital or even a part-time job in a pet store that would help you in your career plans.

                    JANE
I know. But Mom and I have talked about it. And with Lance Drake, my coach, you know. And we think that I'll never have the opportunity again. Either I do it now, or forget about it forever. I think my Dad would have wanted me to try it.

                    DEAN
And you, Louise?

                    LOUISE
Her father was one of the top players in the country. Jane thought a lot of him and still thinks a lot about him. We all want Jane to go to college, but that's something she can always do, a little later on. These things only come once. And I plan to travel with her, so I'll keep an eye on her studies and give her companionship.

                    DEAN
    Well, all right, then. I'll talk to
    your teachers about setting up a
    study away from home program. Jane,
    we'll all be rooting for you here at
    Laguna High.

SCHOOL CORRIDOR

Jane and Louis come out of the door of the
dean's office.

Roger is with another boy, PETE and girl,
BERNICE. They are talking together. Roger
looks up and spots Jane. He waves.

                    JANE
    Oh, Mom, there's Roger. Excuse me
    for a minute.

Jane joins the group.

                    JANE
    So, how're you guys doing?

                    ROGER
    You know Pete, I'm not sure if you
    know Bernice. Bernice Sanderson.
    She's new here. We went to the Prom
    together. Neither of us could find a
    date.

                    JANE
    Hi.

ROGER
Wow, you're look'n good, Jane. We
read about you in the paper. That
match with Campbell. We're so proud.

JANE
Well, thanks. We were just in
talking to the Dean and it looks
like I'm going to be playing on the
junior tour the rest of the year.

ROGER
You mean you won't be in school?
You'll be away?

JANE
Oh, I'll be home on weekends . . .
and holidays, I guess . . . and
between matches.

PETE
We'll miss you, Jane.

JANE
Oh, you just cheer for me.

ROGER
Gosh, Jane, are you free Friday
night? I'd sure like to see you.
Maybe we could go over to Schraft's
for a soda?

JANE
That's really nice, Roger. But
Friday I've got to pack. We're going
to be leaving for Las Vegas in the
morning.

                    ROGER
        Wow. Well, I mean OK. But call me.

                    JANE
        I will.

Jane walks back to Louise, and turns to wave
goodbye.

JANE P.O.V.—LOOKING BACK

Roger has already turned back and is talking
with Bernice.

EXT. LAS VEGAS—MIRAGE HOTEL TENNIS COURT—DAY

BANNER: 15th ANNUAL WALDBAUM CUP
Jane serves. MARTINA O'HAGAN, a blonde
bombshell with small upturned breasts and
sporting tiny pearl earrings and several
gold rings on her fingers, returns the ball.
An advertisement for Waldbaum's supermarket
chain is on the far wall.

Jane and Martina hit the ball back and forth.

Jane snaps rapier returns.

O'Hagan's return sails into the net.

Crowd applauds as Jane takes a point.

INSET
- - - - - - - -
SCOREBOARD

	Game
Bennington	15
O'Hagan	0

- - - - - - - - -

INT. PRESS BOOTH—DAY

> CHARLEY
> The first day of the Waldbaum Cup
> here in Las Vegas is turning out to
> be a lucky day for Jane Bennington.

> CHRIS
> It's more than luck, Charley. This
> girl plays a terrific game. She got
> strength, accuracy, confidence and
> style. Those are all the ingredients
> for greatness. She reminds me of
> Anna Kornikova when she first went on
> the tour.

COURT

CAMERA is behind Martina as she runs after a
ball and pounds it back to Jane. It is a high
blooper. Jane slams the ball across court,
where Martina can't reach it.

INSET

- - - - - - - - - -

SCOREBOARD

	Set 1	Set 2
Bennington	6	6
O'Hagan	3	4

- - - - - - - - - - -

CROWD CHEERING

LOUISE AND LANCE IN STANDS CHEERING

COURT

Jane holds a silver trophy in her arms. A TV camera focuses on her.

> EXECUTIVE
> It's a great pleasure to present you with this check for eighty thousand dollars from Waldbaum's, the supermarket chain where shoppers get cents off deals every day of the week.

He hands Jane the check. She smiles and holds the check up for Louise, who is off to the side of the circle, to see.

EXT./ INT. AIRPLANE IN AIR—DAY

Louis and Jane are seated next to each other. Jane is studying a schoolbook. Louise is reading a Glamour magazine.

EXT. DALLAS HOTEL FRONT—DAY

BANNER—"NIKE OPEN"

CROWD

COURT

Jane is bobbing up and down. Sweat is pouring off her. She is all intense concentration.

APHRODITE BALTIMORE wipes perspiration from brow, bounces the ball several times and serves. She is a large black muscular teenager, 6'4", with hair braided in white beads, an athletic Amazon. She is swathed in a dark blue, single-piece nylon tennis outfit.

CAMERA PANS behind Jane as she runs for the ball and returns it smartly.

Baltimore runs across court and hits the ball back.

Jane hits the ball back.

Aphrodite dashes after ball across court but can't get to it in time.

INSET
- - - - - - - - - - - - - - -
SCORBOARD

	Game	Set 1	Set 2
Bennington	40	6	2
Baltimore	15	1	6

- - - - - - - - - - - - - - -

INSET

- - - - - - - - - - - - - - - - - -

SCORBOARD

	Game	Set 1	Set 2	Set 3
Bennington	0	6	6	4
Baltimore	40	1	2	3

- - - - - - - - - - - - - - - - - -

It is the 6th game of the final set. Jane is down 40-love.

She drills an ace at game point and goes into 5-3 lead. She's escaped the 40-love deficit.

INSET

- - - - - - - - - - - - - - - - - -

SCOREBOARD

	Game	Set 1	Set 2	Set 3
Bennington	0	6	2	5
Baltimore	40	1	6	3

- - - - - - - - - - - - - - - - - -

Aphrodite meekly nets a backhand at break point. Jane wins the victory.

INSET

- - - - - - - - - - - - - - - - - -

SCOREBOARD

	Game	Set 1	Set 2	Set 3
Bennington	60	6	2	6
Baltimore	40	1	6	3

- - - - - - - - - - - - - - - - - -

MEDIUM SHOT—CENTER COURT

Jane and Aphrodite walk to the net and shake hands. Jane goes to the bench and packs up her racquet. The crowd is applauding. Jane goes over to the fans at the side of the fence and signs autographs and tennis balls. She is ecstatic.

INT. CLUB HOUSE BAR—DAY

Lance watches a tennis game replay on the TV behind the bar. He is drinking a whiskey on the rocks. BOBO BASKIN, reporter for the World of Tennis Magazine, taps him on the shoulder. Bobo is wearing a bright plaid blazer, yellow polo shirt and khakis.

Lance turns.

                    BOBO
     Lance Drake, you old son of a gun!
     I thought that was you. What brings
     you out here? I thought you were off
     the tour?

                    LANCE
     If you saw the final, I'm coaching
     Bennington.

                    BOBO
     That was some game. Classic speed
     and agility beats Big Babe tennis.
     Bennington's got style. So, what can
     you tell me about her?

                    LANCE
     She's one to keep an eye on. She's
     got great natural ability, one of
     the finest young players I've ever
     seen. She's making her debut on the
     circuit.

                    BOBO
     Maybe you'll give me an interview
     with her some day?

                    LANCE
     Yeah, sure, Bobo. Any time. Good to
     see you.

INT. AIRPLANE—NIGHT

Jane and Louise sit next to each other. Jane
is studying a schoolbook. Louise is asleep
with a sleep mask over her eyes.

INT. HOTEL ROOM—NIGHT

Jane is sprawled across bed asleep over her
schoolbooks. The light is on.

EXT. KEY BISCAYNE—RESORT—DAY

BANNER—"LIPTON CUP"

CROWD

COURT

Jane is bobbing up and down, sweat is pouring
off her and she is all intense concentration.
Her hair is pushed back behind a white
headband with a Nike logo on it. She is
wearing tiny gold earrings and a slim gold
tennis necklace.

On the other side is BRANDT, bouncy with a
full mane of dark black hair tumbling over
her shoulders from a white headband and soft

toned muscles. She bounces the ball several times and serves.

Jane runs for the ball and smacks it back smartly.

Brandi runs across court and hits the ball back.

Jane's face is fierce as she hits the ball back.

Brandi dashes after ball across the court. She can't get to it.

Jane loses a match point at 6-5 in the third set on what she thinks is a bad call, leading to a tiebreak.

>   REFEREE
> Out!

>   JANE
> No way!

                                    FADE TO:

Then she's one up in the tiebreak and it's Brandi's serve.

INSET
- - - - - - - - - - - - - - - - - -
SCOREBOARD

	Game	Set 1	Set 2	Set 3
Bennington	30	6	7	6
Brandt	40	2	5	6

- - - - - - - - - - - - - - - - - -

Brandi fights off two match points.

INSET

- - - - - - - - - - - - - - -

SCOREBOARD

	Set 1	Set 2	Set 3
Bennington	6	7	7
Brandt	2	5	6

- - - - - - - - - - - - - - -

At match point in the 14th game, Jane sizzles a backhand that just hits inside the line to win.

INSET

- - - - - - - - - - - - - - -

SCOREBOARD

	Set 1	Set 2	Set 3
Bennington	2	7	8
Brandt	6	5	6

- - - - - - - - - - - - - - -

MEDIUM SHOT—CENTER COURT

Jane and Brandi walk to the net and kiss each other on the cheek. Jane goes to bench and packs up racquet. The crowd is applauding. Jane goes over to fans at side of fence and signs autographs and tennis balls. She is smiling.

EXT. MIAMI COUNTRY CLUB—POOLSIDE—DAY

Jane, Lance and Louise are lounging with drinks in deck chairs at a table near the pool. They are in bathing suits.

LANCE

Louise, Jane's got to have an accountant. I can continue to be her manager, but with the amount of winnings, we're going to need someone to look after it. I spoke with Harry Greenfield today. He's an accountant in Los Angeles and handles a lot of sports people. He'll take the account. He's a real good guy.

LOUISE

Whatever you say, Lance. We haven't had so much money in I don't know how long. But can't we just put it in the bank?

LANCE

There's a little more to it than that. I also had a call from the Danny Hiflinger people today. They're looking to put out a new line of tennis skirts, They've had their marketing people out on the circuit looking for good new models. They think Jane's got just the look and the ability to endorse the skirts. She's been gaining a great following and she's becoming very popular with the fans.

JANE

My goodness! Who ever could believe it!

                    LANCE
     So that means we'll have to get a
     lawyer, too. Vito DeLuca. I'll call
     him. To work up the contracts and
     all that, nothing to worry about.
     I'll take care of everything.

                    JANE
     Oh, look! There's Norm Van Trotter.

JANE'S P.O.V.—NORM VAN TROTTER ON THE HIGH
DIVING BOARD

NORM smiles and waves at Jane.

Jane returns the smile with a smile.

Norm runs down the board, bounces on the tip,
does a flip and plunges gracefully into the
pool. He swims over to the side of the pool
where Jane is sitting, gets out of the water
and walks over to the threesome.

                    NORM
     Hi, Jane. Mrs. Bennington. Lance.
     How're you doing?

                    LOUISE
     Just, fine Norm. That was a great
     game you played today. You're
     certainly moving up.

                    NORM
     Not like Jane, though. Hey, Jane,
     Tommy, Alice, Franco, Sandy and
     Hilda and some of the other players
     are at that table on the other side

of the pool, why don't you come over
and join us?

Norm dives into pool with a SPLASH and CAMERA
follows him across the pool. The YOUNG
PLAYERS are sitting around the table in the
distance ahead of him.

                    JANE
        Oh, I don't know. Mom . . .

                    LOUISE
        Sure, Jane, why don't you go ahead
        with the young people. Lance and
        I'll discuss this endorsement stuff.

Jane gets up and walks around the pool to the
other side where she sits down at the table
with the other YOUNG PLAYERS.

                    ALICE
        Hi, Jane. Miami's a lot more
        exciting than some of the other
        places we've been, you ought to join
        us more often. We're all friends off
        the court, you know.

                    JANE
        Well, I've got my Mom with me. And
        My coach.

                    HILDA
        Oh, we all put up with them. My Dad
        comes to watch some of my games. And
        last year, my Mom was with me a lot.
        But they're just not any fun.

ALICE
Sandy, show us your new tennis
bracelet. Hilda says it's gorgeous.

SANDY holds up a very tanned armed upon which
a gold bracelet with diamonds dangles.

SANDY
Can you believe it? Gino De Lorca
gave it to me. At the opening
reception for the tournament the
other night. He's got a great big
house over on Key Biscayne. Said he
admired my playing so much.

HILDA
He's sort of old.

SANDY
Yeah. But he's like an uncle. He's
the head of the Tennis Association.
He knows a lot of people everywhere.

NORM
We're going dancing tomorrow night
after the semi-finals. Down at the
Flamingo Club. Wanna go?

JANE
Gee, that sounds like fun. I haven't
been out in . . . seems like
forever. Let me ask my Mom.

HILDA
Tell her we're going to be
chaperoned, G-d help us. Can't have
all this talent let out of their

cage on their own. Sandy's coach is
going to go with us.

            ALICE
You've just got to go with us. A
bunch from the club here will be
going.

            JANE
I'd like to. I'd really like to.

EXT. TENNIS COURT—DAY

Lance and Louise are watching TWO PLAYERS
practicing on the court.

            LANCE
It would be a good way to meet a lot
of important and influential people.
Not just tennis people. But people
who could be useful to Jane and to
you—rich, famous people.

            LOUISE
Oh, I suppose you're right. But she
shouldn't be off by herself.

            LANCE
Let's face it, Jane's doing well in
school and her game's been getting
better and better. This is just the
beginning. You can't keep her locked
up all the time. She's got to have
some fun with people her age.

            LOUISE
Well, yes, I suppose you're right.

EXT. HOTEL—NIGHT

A large white limousine pulls up to the
hotel's entrance. Norm, Alice, Hilda, Tommy,
Franco, Sandy, Jane and SLADE BENNETT,
Sandy's coach, get into the limo. The limo
driver in a black chauffeur's uniform holds
the door as they file in. They are dressed
in disco clothes. The girls are in skin-
tight strapless microskirts. Jane is in a
short strapless Michael Kors concoction that
swathes her body contours like a glorified Ace
bandage.

Slade calls into the muted glow of the
interior of the limo through the half-opened
door being held by the chauffeur.

                    SLADE
        I'll sit up front.

He slams the door and gets in the front seat.

INSIDE THE LIMO

The inside of the limo is like a softly
lighted cave, with little muted lights
running along the side panels. Soft music is
playing. Norm, Alice and Hilda are in the
back seat. Tommy, Franco, Sandy and Jane are
squeezed into the seat opposite.

                    NORM
        Now this is a little more like it,
        gang.

                    TOMMY
    See if there's anything in the bar
    there.

Norm pulls a side panel and takes out
decanter of bourbon.

Franco pulls open another panel.

                    FRANCO
    Ice and soda here.

He pours drinks for the group.

                    JANE
    No, thanks.

                    HILDA
    Oh, go ahead, Jane. A little drink
    isn't going to hurt anybody. It's
    a good way to let off some steam.
    You should have seen Mary Taggert
    after the Denver Open last year. She
    couldn't have hit a tennis ball if
    it were two inches in front of her
    nose. We need to relax, after all.

                    ALICE
    Anybody want a joint? I've got some
    pot.

                    FRANCO
    Gimme a hit.

EXT. FLAMINGO CLUB—NIGHT

Limo pulls up to front of the club.

Loud disco MUSIC is playing.

DANCE FLOOR

Norm and Jane are dancing very energetically amid other couples swirling around them. The MUSIC is bouncy, energetic and upbeat. Jane's well-shaped body, her small curves, tiny firm breasts and well-toned butt undulate to the music. Jane is having a great time.

INSERT—JANE'S FACE

INSERT—NORM'S FACE

Norm and Jane dance over to the table where the rest of the group is. The table is littered with bottles. Jane and Norm collapse into the banquette seats. Over at the bar, Slade is smoking a cigarette talking with a WOMAN. He has his hand around her waist.

>   ALICE
>   This song by the Stinking Clapboard
>   is awesome.

>   SANDY
>   Bartleby Thump. Boy is he cute.
>   I saw him in the stands at the
>   Michelin Open last year. He invited
>   me backstage. I love these English
>   groups.

EDDIE DI PALMA walks over to the table as the music switches to a SLOW DANCE.

>   EDDIE
>   Jane, let's dance.

Jane rises and goes to the dance floor with EDDIE. They embrace and dance as Jane rests her head on his shoulder.

OUTSIDE THE CLUB

EDDIE kisses Jane as she gets into the limo.

INSERT—TV MONITOR

VISUAL	SOUND
Side view of Jane hitting the ball with a racquet, dancing and swirling.	When I'm playing my best, I want to look my best.
CAMERA ZOOMS in and focuses on Hilfinger label on the side of her tennis skirt.	That's why I choose Hilfinger. Hilfinger, for the young sportswoman on the move.

INT. TV COMMERCIAL SET—DAY

CAMERA PULLS BACK to show Jane smiling in front of the camera. A HAIRSTYLIST and MAKEUP WOMAN come over to Jane. The makeup woman dabs her nose with powder and then touches up her mascara.

> DIRECTOR
> OK. That's the way. One more take to go.

Jane walks off the set. Louise is stunningly decked out in diamond solitaires and a fur coat over a black couture pants suit. She pecks Jane on the cheek.

> LOUISE
> That was so nice. I don't know if
> I'm more proud of you as a tennis
> champ or as an actress.

> JANE
> Aw, Mom, please, you're embarrassing
> me.

> LANCE
> We were just over at the association
> finishing up your summer schedule.
> We've got London, Paris and
> Barcelona.

> JANE
> I thought we were going back to
> California for the summer. We
> haven't been home for months.

> LOUISE
> Darling, we just can't stop now. I
> never thought you'd get this far,
> but you're the sixth seeded player
> in the circuit. We can't afford to
> drop out now.

> JANE
> But, Mom, Roger and all my friends
> are at home.

LOUISE
Come on, Jane. You've never been
to Europe and you know I certainly
haven't. How many of your friends
back home would miss an opportunity
like this. We have plenty of offers
to consider. Here's some of your
mail. Don Johnson's invited you to
do a walk-on part on Miami Vice,
and George Michael, you know him,
the big pop star's invited to take
you out while you're in London.
Lance says it's worth doing for the
publicity.

EXT. LONDON SKYLINE—DAY

EXT. WIMBELDON TENNIS COURTS—DAY

BANNER—"BRITISH JUNIOR OPEN"

The Center Court at Wimbledon overlooked by
the Royal Box, tennis fans in the stands.
MEN in the seats are wearing straw hats and
blazers and WOMEN are wearing big colorful
hats with flowers.

Jane walks by the elegant SABRINA FLORENCIA,
a little bronze goddess who is posing her
youthful beauty before the cameras. OTHER
YOUNG PLAYERS are signing autographs and
exulting in the glamour of exhibiting their
golden well-toned limbs and soft athleticism
for the paparazzi.

CENTER COURT

Jane is facing JANA NAZDROVIA, a slim, leggy Russian with a very long braided ponytail, a frisky young colt with long legs and an athletic body, her trim young tanned legs come out from a thigh-high tennis skirt.

Jane is bobbing up and down, all intense concentration.

The willowy Russian wipes perspiration from brow, bounces the ball several times, stretches high into the air and serves.

Jane returns the serve.

Jana snaps away her shots. She slashes one double-hander after another with surgical power. Jane's forehand is ineffectual.

Jana easily takes Jane's serves. She returns them viciously. Jane is forced to step backward to try to corral them.

Jana strides to the baseline, putting a ball into her skirt pocket. As she puts a service ball into her skirt pocket, her short tennis skirt hikes, as does her panties, revealing a firm, shapely round bottom.

BOX IN THE STANDS—BOBO AND LANCE

                    BOBO
          Gotta love that ass!

                    LANCE
          A great body. Like the model on the
          cereal box that makes you shit good.

                    LANCE
     That, my friend, is what makes this
     such a great sport.

COURT

Nazdrovia keeps attacking Jane with a mean-
spirited backhand return, shoving Jane into
a corner and rendering her helpless. Jana
follows up with a backhand drop shot that
lands and expires on command.

INSET
- - - - - - - -
SCOREBOARD
           Set 1
Bennington   0
Nazdrovia   6
- - - - - - - - -

Jane is in her changeover chair. She is
sweating profusely. She wipes perspiration
off with a towel.

                    JANE
               (to herself)
     Gotta calm down, Jane, and get
     control.

Jane wins her first game since the third game
of the opening set.

INSET
- - - - - - - - - - - - - - -
SCOREBOARD
        Set 1 Set 2 Set 3
Bennington   0   1
Nazdrovia   6   1
- - - - - - - - - - - - - - -

They rally.

INSET
- - - - - - - - - - - - - - -
SCOREBOARD
        Set 1 Set 2 Set 3
Bennington   0   2
Nazdrovia   6   1
- - - - - - - - - - - - - - -

Jane breaks Jana to take a 2-1 lead. Jane
marches back to her chair and slams down her
racquet.

                JANE
            (to herself)
     That's the way. Now I'll show her.

Their shots fly across the net with harmful
intent. The groundstrokes burn like lasers.
Their serves detonate on delivery.

INT. PRESS BOX

CHRIS HORNSBY is behind the microphone.

             HORNSBY
    It looks as though Bennington is
    trying to play off Nazdrovia's

backhand. She's been working on it.
And it seems to be paying off.

                    CHRIS
It's really amazing to think
that just under a year ago, Jane
Bennington was playing high school
tennis in California and today she's
here at the British Junior Open
within striking distance of beating
Kate Stolfoos in the semi-finals.

                    HORNSBY
No question about it, Chris, it's
a young person's game. Now the big
question everyone is asking is
will she have the stamina and the
endurance to go the whole way?

Jane is sweating heavily. She serves.

Jane breaks Jana for a 5-4 lead.

INSET
- - - - - - - - - - - - - - -
SCOREBOARD

	Set 1	Set 2	Set 3
Bennington	0	6	5
Nazdrovia	6	4	4

- - - - - - - - - - - - - - -

Jana blows on her fingertips. She serves.

Jane returns a forehand missile. It sails
past Jana.

INSET

- - - - - - - - - - - - - - - -

SCOREBOARD

	Set 1	Set 2	Set 3
Bennington	0	6	6
Nazdrovia	6	4	4

- - - - - - - - - - - - - - -

Jane raises both arms to celebrate the victory.

INT. PRESS CONFERENCE—DAY

Jane and Jana are at a long table with microphones in front of them. Jane has a large crystal dish in front of her, while a silver trophy is in front of Jana. PAPARAZZI are sitting on the floor in front of the assembled press and off to the sides. FLASHBULBS are popping.

> REPORTER ONE
> Jane, what are your next plans?

> JANE
> To go to the U.S. Open next month.
> I'm anxious to get back to the
> United States.

> REPORTER TWO
> Jana, how does it feel to be voted
> the sexiest legs in tennis by the
> Tennis Fans Association?

> JANA
> Someday, after tennis, I hope to be
> in the movies. So I guess it's OK.

But I'd rather be appreciated for my
game.

> REPORTER THREE
> Jane, is there any truth to the
> rumor that you got an offer from
> Playboy to pose nude?

> JANE
> I don't care how much they would pay
> me. I'll keep my clothes on.

> REPORTER FOUR
> Jana, what about you?

> JANA
> If it would help my movie career one
> day, who's to say?

> REPORTER FIVE
> You've been seen with Boris Nemosky,
> the ice hockey goalie. Any truth to
> the rumor you're going steady?

> JANA
> We're good friends, yes.

EXT./INT. LONDON—HIPPODROME NIGHT CLUB—NIGHT

Jane is celebrating. She is in a tight black
miniskirt. She is dancing up a storm with a
MAN.

INT. HOTEL JANE'S ROOM—LONDON—DAY

ALARM CLOCK buzzes at 10 A.M.

Jane unburies herself from the mound of blankets she's been sleeping under. She still has the same clothes on from the night before. She slips out of her clothes and walks to the shower.

Jane's nude silhouette against the steamy shower door.

Jane steps from the shower, takes a bath towel and starts to dry herself. She walks to the window.

> JANE
> Shriek! Oh my God!

Framed in the window is a PAPARAZZI with cameras and lenses strung around his neck pointing a camera at her. He is standing on a scaffold.

Jane pulls down the window blind on him.

BLACK

EXT. PRIVATE GULFSTREAM AIRPLANE—DAY

The great expanse of the Los Angeles Basin.

EXT. LAGUNA HILLS, CALIFORNIA—ALICIA PARKWAY—DAY

A huge long white BANNER with the inscription in blue "WELCOME HOME, JANE" is carried in front of the band by two majorettes. CROWDS line the roadway, which has been sealed off by police. Blue and white bunting and balloons hang from the lampposts along the way. The MARCHING BAND is playing LOUD MUSIC with lots of brass and drums.

Behind the high school band are CHEERLEADERS dressed in white tennis skirts and sweaters, jumping up and down and doing cartwheels. An honor guard of policemen carrying the California and United States flags marches behind.

Then follows a white Cadillac convertible festooned with flowers. Jane sits on top of the back seat. Louise and Roger are on each side.

The crowd CHEERS and waves as Jane goes by.

EXT. LAGUNA NIGUEL PARK—DAY

Jane stands on a raised platform in front of the crowd assembled in the park. Sharing the platform with her at a microphone is MAYOR JOE HATFIELD, a heavyset man in a blue blazer, checkered shirt and grey trousers.

>   MAYOR HATFIELD
> Jane, you've brought great
> distinction and notoriety to our
> town. All of us are so proud of
> your accomplishments. As a gesture
> of our pride and esteem, we want to
> present you with this new Camero
> sports car, which, you will see, is
> filled with tennis balls. We also
> know, as a California girl, of your
> love for animals. So we take extra
> special pleasure in presenting you
> with this Arabian horse, which will

be boarded at the county stables
at county expense for you to use
whenever you're back here with all
your friends and family.

A middle-aged WOMAN in a white cowboy skirt
and hat leads a golden steed by the reins to
the edge of the platform. Jane walks over and
pets it.

                    JANE
          Oh, I don't know what to say. I'm
          speechless.

                    MAYOR HATFIELD
          No need to say anything, Jane,
          because we also have one other
          little present for you: this pure
          bred Schnauzer, from Laguna Puppy
          Farms.

A grey, bearded Schnauzer is let off its
leash at the end of the platform and comes
running to Jane and bounds into her arms.

                    JANE
          Oh, thank you, thank you, thank you.
          This just has to be the happiest day
          of my life.

INT. ANTONELLO'S RESTAURANT—NIGHT

Jane, Louise and Lance are seated at a table
in a luxurious private dinning room in the
fashionable Antonello's Restaurant. The
waiter is pouring red wine into wide glass
goblets. Jane is dressed head-to-toe in
Armani.

MARTY BELCHER, representative of the Dunlop sporting Goods Company, is seated with them. He hands Jane a gold bracelet studded with diamonds.

                    BELCHER
     Jane, this bracelet has a diamond
     for every tournament you've won so
     far. It's valued at $150,000. Dunlop
     Tennis wants you to have it as a
     reminder of how much we value you,
     and want you to become a member
     of our company and endorse Dunlop
     products.

He hands her a contract.

                    BELCHER (contd.)
     Of course, there's a nice lucrative
     contract, too. We want you to
     seriously consider endorsing Dunlop
     racquets. All the details are
     spelled out in this contract. You
     can go over it with your manager
     here, Mr. Drake.

They all click glasses.

ESTABLISHING—NEW YORK SKYLINE

Jane is posing in front of a PHOTOGRAPHER for a glamour photo for a magazine. NAOMI CAMPELL, the supermodel, walks off an adjoining set where she's been posing for a swimsuit calendar, wearing a long sweater over a bikini.

> PHOTOGRAPHER
> Jane, do you know my most favorite
> model, Naomi Campell?

> JANE
> Oh, my goodness! Naomi Campell! Who
> doesn't know Naomi Campell?

> NAOMI
> And what kind of tennis fan would
> I be if I didn't recognize the
> marvelous Jane Bennington? Jane,
> we're having a little get-together,
> a cocktail party, over at my place
> tonight. Why don't you come over
> and we'll get to know one another a
> little better.

> JANE
> Gosh, that would be great!

> NAOMI
> My assistant will call you later
> with the address and directions.

EXT. FLUSHING MEADOW—ARTHUR ASHE STADIUM—DAY

SIGN—"U.S. OPEN SEMI-FINALS"

Jane bobs up and down.

Across the court is her opponent, DOMINIQUE
SCHILLER, an athletic German lilliput with
short dirty blond hair and well-shaped bones.
She wipes perspiration from her brow, bounces
the ball several times and serves.

INSET
- - - - - - - -
SCOREBOARD
            Set 1
Bennington   5
Schiller   6
- - - - - - - -

Dominique blasts an ace. A LINESPERSON calls it. Dominique complains. The UMPIRE stands by the call.

INSET
- - - - - - - -
SCOREBOARD
            Set 1
Bennington   6
Schiller   6
- - - - - - - -

The line call distracts Dominique. The first set goes to Jane.

INSET
- - - - - - - -
SCOREBOARD
            Set 1
Bennington   7
Schiller   6
- - - - - - - -

But Dominique is not beaten. She rallies and sweeps through the second set without the loss of a game. Jane has no answer for her flood of winners.

INSET

- - - - - - - - - - - - - - -

SCOREBOARD

	Set 1	Set 2	Set 3
Bennington	7	0	
Schiller	6	6	

- - - - - - - - - - - - - - -

Jane isn't put off. A tense moment in the third set: Dominique has a break point in the third game.

INSET

- - - - - - - - - - - - - - -

SCOREBOARD

	Set 1	Set 2	Set 3
Bennington	7	0	0
Schiller	6	6	3

- - - - - - - - - - - - - - -

Jane eventually breaks in the fourth game and Dominique, now physically spent, has no more to give. Eight minutes short of two hours, Dominique nets a forehand, handing Jane a 7-6, 0-6, 6-3 triumph.

INSET

- - - - - - - - - - - - - - -

SCOREBOARD

	Set 1	Set 2	Set 3
Bennington	7	0	6
Schiller	6	6	3

- - - - - - - - - - - - - - -

Jane jumps for joy. She covers her face with her hands.

She runs across the court to hug her mother and Lance in their courtside box.

CENTER COURT

Jane gives Dominique a warm embrace at the net.

Then Jane throws some of her racquets into the stands, screaming happily.

INT. CONFERENCE ROOM—DAY

The room is crowded with reporters. DOMINIQUE and JANE are behind microphones at a table in the front.

> REPORTER ONE
> What was the deciding factor in the match?

> JANE
> I paced myself. I got a second or maybe third wind halfway through the third set. That's when I started to run my games. It was a long match.

> REPORTER TWO
> How do you feel going into the final?

> JANE
> It's this type of game that inspires me. Dominique is a terrific opponent.

> REPORTER THREE
> We know you wanted to make it to the final round this year, Dominique.

This broke your winning streak. Any
comments?

                    DOMINQUE
Actually, I feel very good. That's
the best game I've played that I
lost. I've been playing very well
all year. All I know is that I
played a good tournament and I
should be happy.

                    REPORTER FOUR
How do you like New York, Jane?

                    JANE
New York's an exciting city. But
I plan to rest up before Sunday's
match.

EXT. REGINE'S NIGHTCLUB—NIGHT

Jane and Claudia are on the dance floor with
two very suave MEN in polo shirts and sports
jackets. The MUSIC is LOUD.

Jane and Claudia walking down Fifth Avenue,
arm in arm, two sisters laughing and giggling
to themselves.

EXT. ARTHUR ASHE STADIUM—DAY

SUPER—"U.S. OPEN TENNIS FINAL, FLUSHING
MEADOW, N.Y."

Jane bobs up and down. She is all intense
concentration.

Across the court, KATE STOLFOOS, a lithe Norwegian with straight pointed breasts and sturdy legs.

INSET
- - - - - - - - - - - - - - -
SCOREBOARD

	Set 1	Set 2	Set 3
Bennington	6	4	
Stolfoos	4	6	
- - - - - - - - - - - - - - -

They trade sets. Kate looks as if she'll walk away with the win when she has a break up in the third and leading 5-3.

Sweat pours off Jane.

INSET
- - - - - - - - - - - - - - -
SCOREBOARD

	Set 1	Set 2	Set 3
Bennington	6	4	3
Stolfoos	4	6	5

- - - - - - - - - - - - - - -

Jane holds serve to make it 5-4 in Kate's favor and then Kate serves for the match.

INSET
- - - - - - - - - - - - - - -
SCOREBOARD

	Set 1	Set 2	Set 3
Bennington	6	4	4
Stolfoos	4	6	5
- - - - - - - - - - - - - - -

Jane's not going to give up without one hell
of a fight. She breaks Kate to level the match
at 5-5. The balance of fortune had changed.

INSET
- - - - - - - -
SCOREBOARD

Set 3
Bennington   5
Stolfoos   5

- - - - - - - -

INSET
- - - - - - - -
SCOREBOARD

Set 3
Bennington   6
Stolfoos   5
- - - - - - - -

Kate serves. She double-faults. She gives
Jane her first Grand Slam title.

INSET
- - - - - - - - - - - - - -
SCOREBOARD

	Set 1	Set 2	Set 3
Bennington	6	4	7
Stolfoos	4	6	5
- - - - - - - - - - - - - -

Jane runs over to Louise for the customary
kiss.

CENTER COURT

Jane and Kate walk to the net and shake hands. CAMERA follows as Jane goes to bench and packs up racquet. The CROWD is applauding. Jane goes overt to fans at side of fence and sign autographs and tennis balls. She's smiling.

SIDE COURT

> CHRIS
> Jane, how does it feel to win your first Grand Slam event?

> JANE
> It's like a dream. I feel incredible.

EXT. LONDON—MAYFAIR HOTEL—NIGHT

THE GUESTS, people in the tuxedos and ball gowns, are greeted in the lobby by a carefully clipped bearded MAN with in a tux, a medal and sash across his middle.

The guests file past a SIGN in front of the ballroom that reads "BRITISH INVITATIONAL RECEPTION AND DINNER" and on into the ballroom.

Jane is decked out in a short low-cut black and red taffeta number that she is practically falling out of when she runs into Eddie di Palma.

> JANE
> My goodness, what are you doing here?

                    EDDIE DI PALMA
My Dad has business here. He knows
I like tennis and he asked me if
I wanted to come along with him.
While he's at work, I can watch the
matches.

                    JANE
Gee, it's so good seeing you again.

                    EDDIE
Can I see you after dinner? Let's
go dancing like we did in Miami.
London's an exciting city. I've been
here before. There're lots of clubs.

Louise comes over with a short, dark haired
man in a tuxedo, smoking a cigar.

                    LOUISE
Hymie, meet Jane, my daughter. I'm
so proud of her. Hymie is a member
of the Rothschild family, Jane. And
he's been telling me all about his
investment banking business and his
horses. He races them.

                    JANE
This is my friend, Eddie Di Palma.
My mother.

                    LOUISE
And Hymie.

                    HYMIE
Di Palma. Any relation to Donald Di
Palma? He built Robin's Nest Wharf
here in London, not to mention Di

Palma Tower in New York. Here kid,
have a cigar.

                    EDDIE
Thanks, but no thanks. I can't stand
those things. I keep telling my
father to throw those things out.
They're antediluvian, from another
age.

                    HYMIE
Hard to teach an old dog new tricks.
Come on, Louise, there's Sir
Wilfred. I want you and Jane to meet
him. You'll excuse us son?

                    EDDIE
Sure. I'll see you later Jane?

                    JANE
Yes.

DINNER TABLE

CAMERA PANS waiters as they bring silvered-
covered plates to the table and unveil large
lobsters underneath.

Jane eats lobster and talks to the PEOPLE
next to her.

WAITER pours wine for Louise as Hymie feeds
her a piece of lobster.

CAMERA pans DIGNITARIES sitting at the front
table. It rests on CHAUNCEY DEPEW, head of
the British Tennis Association, as he rises
to the podium at the center of table.

                    CHAUNCEY
In England we have a long and
proud tradition of tennis. The
young people we are honoring here
tonight are the proud future of that
tradition. They represent the best
for which tennis stands: agility,
athletic prowess, the desire to do
better and, of course, that without
which any sport can endure, honor
and integrity.

EXT. DIONYSIS CLUB—NIGHT

Eddie and Jane are at a table with drinks.
The vast crowd dances to a D.J.

                    EDDIE
You look marvelous, Jane. I saw you
on television. I'm so glad you could
come out.

                    JANE
Well, Eddie so am I. Mom says
there's not too much to do until
we get to Paris. I think she wants
to get away from me. This has been
awfully hard on her. She's been
travelling with me, and she hardly
has had any time for herself.

                    EDDIE
I saw the way she was getting along
with Hymie. I don't think she'll
miss you. Let's go back to my hotel.
Dad's got me a suite there. We can
listen to music or watch some TV.

                    JANE
Well, sure, that sounds like fun.
I'm not sure I like all these people
around me all the time.

INT. HOTEL ROOM—NIGHT

Jane tours the room as she and Eddie enter.
Jane picks up a book lying open on a coffee
table.

                    JANE
What's this?

                    EDDIE
One of my books from school.

                    JANE
"Naked Lunch." What a strange name
for a book.

                    EDDIE
It's all about a person who creates
a whole world for himself.

                    JANE
I wish I had more time to study. So
many things have happened. I haven't
been able to keep up with all of it.

                    EDDIE
What do you mean? You're a star.
A champ. You can hardly pick up a
magazine or newspaper without seeing
you in it, or someone talking about
you on TV.

Eddie embraces Jane and they kiss.

INT. RESTAURANT—DAY

Hymie and Louise eat breakfast at the table.

>   HYMIE
> You kids should stick with me. I
> know everybody in this town. I
> know everybody in tennis. God, how
> much have I given to the tennis
> association. Sponsorships, boxes,
> prizes. I could do a lot for you,
> Louise.

>   LOUISE
> I don't know what we would have done
> without Lance. He's been so good to
> us.

>   HYMIE
> Oh, yeah, Lance. Well let me tell
> you something about him, about good
> old Lance. One of the best there
> ever was. Problem was the high life,
> the booze, and the girls. Yes,
> the girls. Got too greedy. How do
> you think the twelfth seeded play
> goes from being a major contender
> to a pro at a second rate club
> in California. I'll tell ya'h.
> Too much booze, too many broads,
> too much thinking about money and
> endorsements. He could have been
> great all right, but he's looking
> for a comeback. Not on his own
> account, but someone else's, Jane
> and yours.

                    LOUISE
     Oh, Hymie. I know you mean well.

                    HYMIE
     No, Louise, I haven't felt like
     this in a long time. I could just
     sit here and say you're one of the
     loveliest and most gentle women I've
     met in a long time. Or I could just
     keep quiet. But I'm tellin' ya'h, he
     ain't what you think. Ask anybody.

He leans over and kisses Louise.

INT. HOTEL ROOM—LATER

They are making love on the couch. An empty
bottle of bourbon, several soda cans and
glasses are on the coffee table in front of
them.

EXT. AIR FRANCE AIRPLANE—LANDING STRIP—DAY

EXT. PARIS SKYLINE—EIFFEL TOWER—DAY

EXT. PRIVATE GULFSTREAM—JET LANDING—DAY

Big white stretch limo pulls up to the stairs
at the door of the plane. Jane, Louise and
Lance come down the stairs. Jane is wearing
jeans and a T-shirt. Louise is in a Givenchy
pants suit. Jane is holding the Schnauzer.
They get into the limo, the back door held
open by the chauffeur.

JANE'S P.O.V.—LOOKING OUT THE LIMO WINDOW

Sidewalk shots of Paris, cafes, bistros, etc.

A newsstand with papers on a metal display rack. She can see the front page:

LE MONDE FRENCH NEWSPAPER HEADLINE—"AMERICAN JANE BENNINGTON CHALLENGES CLAIRE LA ROUSSE IN TENNIS OPEN"

Jane watches YOUNG LOVERS holding hands, FAMILIES STROLLING in a park, a flower kiosk with a COUPLE buying a bouquet of flowers, a street MUSICIAN playing an accordion, a COUPLE kissing.

EXT. PARIS HOTEL—DAY

The Limo pulls up to door. Doorman opens door. They step out, go through the hotel door and into the lobby.

INT. HOTEL SUITE—DAY

Jane enters the luxurious suite.

CAMERA PANS as she walks through the suite. She walks to a coffee table in the living room, where a large vase of flowers sits. She takes a card from the vase and reads it aloud.

> JANE
> "Welcome to the French Open. Your suite is courtesy of Adidas sneakers and sporting wear."

She walks into the bathroom, where she exclaims.

                    JANE (contd.)
    "Wow, Mom, look at this."

The bathroom is immense, taken up by a
swimming pool-sized marble tub. It faces a
large window with the skyline of Paris.

                    LOUISE (V.O.)
    Oh, my!

                    JANE
    And one of the other rooms has
    exercise equipment in it. I'm going
    to take a swim right here and then
    go work out.

She takes off her jeans and T-shirt and jumps
into the pool in her panties and bra. She
splashes Louise.

Louise exits.

JANE SWIMMING

EXT. ROLAND GARROS STADIUM—DAY

FANS seeking autographs and paparazzi firing
flashbulbs gather around Jane as she heads
into the court.

CAMERA PANS as Jane, with duffel bag and two
racquets, strides onto the court and sits
down in her chair.

CLAIRE LA ROUSSE, a frisky, budding beauty
with trim tanned legs and small tight-toned
rump set out from a thigh-high white tennis
skirt, wields a Gucci-designed racquet. A

slim gold Rolex adorns her left wrist. An Evian logo adorns the sleeve of her jersey.

In the first game, Jane hits double faults, and then double faults again.

INSET
- - - - - - - -
SCOREBOARD

	Game
Bennington	0
La Rousse	30

- - - - - - - -

Claire serves.

They rally. Claire makes a backhand miss. She lets out a high piercing SHRIEK.

She makes a second backhand fault. She SHRIEKS again.

INSET
- - - - - - - - - - -
SCOREBOARD

	Game	Set 1
Bennington	3	0
La Rousse	0	1

- - - - - - - - - - -

In the seventh game, first set, Jane converts break point with an overhead to go 4-3.

INSET
- - - - - - - - - -
SCOREBOARD

	Game	Set 1
Bennington	15	4
La Rousse	30	3

- - - - - - - - - - -

Jane makes a lunging forehand volley. Claire pumps a forehand return into the net.

INSET
- - - - - - - -
SCOREBOARD

	Set 1
Bennington	6
La Rousse	3

- - - - - - - -

INSET
- - - - - - - - - - -
SCOREBOARD

	Game	Set 1
Bennington	40	6
La Rousse	15	3

- - - - - - - - - - -

It's the first game of the second set. Jane, perspiring heavily, bounces the ball several times and serves.

Jane slams an overhead.

                    JANE
     (hisses)
     Yes . . .

INSET
- - - - - - - - - - -
SCOREBOARD
         Set 1 Set 2
Bennington 6   3
La Rousse   3   3

- - - - - - - - - - -

Claire serves. She double faults.

She serves again. Another double fault.

They rally. Jane wins with a backhand.

INSET
- - - - - - - - - - -
SCOREBOARD
         Set 1 Set 2
Bennington 6   4
La Rousse   3   3
- - - - - - - - - - -

Jane serves for the second set.

She hits a forehand into the net on Claire's
break opportunity. Claire leads.

INSET
- - - - - - - - - - -
SCOREBOARD
         Set 1 Set 2
Bennington 6   5
La Rousse   3   6
- - - - - - - - - - -

Jane forces a tiebreaker.

INSET

- - - - - - - - - - -

SCOREBOARD

	Set 1	Set 2
Bennington	6	6
La Rousse	3	6

- - - - - - - - - - -

Jane serves fast.

Claire makes a stream of errors.

Jane delivers a magnificent lunging backhand that gives her first match point.

Claire, all sweaty, serves.

Jane's forehand return goes wide.

INSET

- - - - - - - - - - - - -

SCOREBOARD

	Set 1	Set 2	Set 3
Bennington	6	4	6
La Rousse	3	6	6

- - - - - - - - - - - - - -

Claire serves.

CAMERA PANS behind Jane as she runs for the ball and returns an un-returnable forehand that coasts down the sideline to win the tiebreaker match.

JANE'S P.O.V.—LOOKING AT COURT

The ball bounces and sails past Claire.

INSET
- - - - - - - - - - - - - - -
SCOREBOARD
          Set 1 Set 2 Set 3
Bennington   6   4   7
La Rousse   3   6   6
- - - - - - - - - - - - - - -

Jane falls to her knees and bursts into
tears.

CENTER COURT

CAMERA FOLLOWS as Jane gets up, briskly runs
to the net and embraces Claire. Then she
scampers into the stands to embrace Lance
and Louise. Then hustles back down to the
court, where a red rug has been lain and the
DUCHESS OF BURGUNDY and TOURNAMENT OFFICIALS,
including YVES CHAMBORD, head of the French
Tennis Association, await her. The CROWD is
applauding.

The Duchess, who has short blond hair and who
is wearing a canary yellow suit and round
gold earrings, clasps Jane's hands in hers.

                    CHAMBORD
          A great game played by two great
          competitors.

                    CLAIRE
          I, of course, do not prefer to lose,
          but if I must lose, then I am happy
          to say that I have lost to a real
          champion of the court, Jane.

                    JANE
Winning and losing isn't as
important as the game itself.
Claire played a tremendous game and
I'm proud to say that we could play
together.

                   CHAMBORD
It's my esteemed pleasure to
introduce the Duchess of Burgundy
who will present the tournament
trophy.

The DUCHESS takes a large silver plate from
an attendant and hands it to Jane, who is
quivering.

                    DUCHESS
On behalf of the tournament, the
sponsor of the tournament, Viva
Spring Water, which so graciously
put up the prize money, and on
behalf of the people of France,
I present you with the winner's
trophy.

She kisses Jane on both cheeks.

                 DUCHESS (contd.)
I am so proud of you, dear.

Jane takes the plate, raises it high over her
head. She cries some more.

Claire pops open bottle of champagne and
sprays it over Jane. Jane takes the bottle
from her and sprays her with the rest of it.

MOVIE MARQUEE SIGN—"TOUJOURS L'AMOUR PREMIERE"

Black limousines pull up to the entranceways of the sidewalk in front of the theatre. The crowd on both sides is roped off with a cordon. FLASHBULBS pop as PAPARRAZI photograph the arriving GLITTERATI, movie stars and other celebrities. A limousine pulls up and out of its interior comes a strikingly handsome young movie star, BLAINE PASCAL, in a tuxedo. He helps Jane, who is wearing a thin, long, low-cut gold gown, out of the limo. Blain and Jane make their way up the walks, stopping on the way to sign photographs.

> FAN ONE
> (to Blaine, handing him a photo)
> I loved you in <u>Love under the Stars.</u>

> FAN TWO
> (to Jane, holding an autograph book)
> Could you sign this "To Beatrice"?

> FAN THREE
> (to Jane)
> "You're the greatest."

Blain and Jane walk in through the theatre doors.

EXT. CHAMPS ELYSEE—DAY

Jane and Louise window shop on the Champs Elysee. They are elegantly dressed and carrying bags from several fashionable stores. They are walking the Schnauzer. They go by a widow display with a big photo of Jane advertising a tennis shirt.A FAN stops Jane on the street and asks for an autograph.

EXT. CANNES HARBOR—DAY

The day is sparkling clear on the Mediterranean. Yachts are moored on the blue sea.

EXT. DECK OF YACHT OF MOMIR EL FASAD—DAY

There is an afternoon party aboard the Yacht "Timor," owned by the multi-millionaire department store merchant MOMIR EL FASAD. MUSIC is playing from the speakers on the ship. SEVERAL young nubile girls and young men, European debutantes, movie stars and Euro-Trash are on the boat, sunning themselves, playing paddle tennis, drinking, laughing, talking. Some are topless. Momir is showing Louise the pilothouse. Jane is at the back of the boat, reading a mathematics textbook. A ball comes flying and hits the book. Jane looks up and sees JEAN CLAUDE BEAUMONT, a handsome young man bronzed tan in a slim Speedo bathing suit coming toward her. He sits down next to her.

                    JEAN CLAUDE
        A day like this is too beautiful to
        spend reading. It must be a very
        good book.

He takes it from her and looks at it.

                    JEAN CLAUDE (contd.)
        "Advanced Algebra."

                    JANE
     The content is solid, but the plot
     leaves something to be desired.

Jane smiles.

                  JANE (contd.)
     I need to study. I haven't studied
     in weeks.

                  JEAN CLAUDE
     Take a break. Life isn't so serious.
     Come and join the others. All work
     and no play makes Jane a dull girl.

Jane hesitates a moment. She throws the book
over the side of the boat.

EXT. DECK OF YACHT OF MOMIR EL FASAD—LATER

Jane is seated at the back of the boat with
Jean Claude and several of the young people.
They are drinking glasses of white wine being
served by a WAITRESS. MUSIC is playing.

The young couples are dancing. Jane is
drinking more white wine. She gets up and
dances. She is becoming tipsy.

UPPER DECK

Louise and Momir are dressed for the evening.
Momir is in a tuxedo with a red carnation.
Louise is in a glittering evening dress, and
wearing a brilliant diamond necklace.

MOMIR
(yelling to lower deck)
We are going to try our hand at the
casino. You young people have a good
time.

Small cutter from the boat carries Momir and
Louise over the blue ocean toward the sunset
skyline of the casinos and hotels of Cannes.

The young people go into the cabin.

INT. CABIN

The interior of the cabin is dimly light.
Wild jazz MUSIC is playing on the interior
stereos. Jean Claude pours whiskey into
glasses. Then he offers pills from a bottle,
which everyone takes. They dance wildly,
with the girls stripping off the bottoms of
their bikinis. Jane takes off her top as an
orgy begins. A couple begins kissing on the
couch. Others pair off and go into separate
rooms of the boat. Jean Claude and Jane go
into a stateroom. Jane lies down on the bed.
Jean Paul kisses her on the mouth and then
the breasts and then slips off her bikini
bottoms. They go into a passionate embrace.

INT. HOTEL ROOM—NIGHT

Louise enters the room. She is quite tipsy.
Jane is asleep in bed. The light is half on.
Louise sits on the side of the sleeping Jane.
She runs her hand over Jane's hair in a very
motherly way.

EXT. BARCLONA TENNIS CLUB—DAY

Fans stream into the court through the gates.

SIGN—"EUROPEAN CHAMPIONSHIPS"

The stadium has a full crowd.

Louise and Lance take seats in the stands.

INT. DRESSING ROOM—DAY

Jane is dressing for the game in front of an open locker. She takes out a bottle of pills and swallows several.

She faces CONCHITA ARROYO-RODRIGUEZ, a dark-haired Latin beauty with dark fiery eyes who is known as the Barcelona Hot Pepper, for her speed, agility and bubbly personality.

Jane wipes perspiration from brow, bounces the ball several times and serves.

Jane runs for the ball and drills it back.

CONCHITA scampers across the court and hits the ball back.

Jane serves to lead 2-1 in the first set. Conchita Arroyo-Rodriguez makes her work extremely hard for every point.

```
INSET
- - - - - - - - - - - - -
SCOREBOARD
                     Set 1
Bennington            2
Arroyo-Rodriguez      1
- - - - - - - - - - - - - -
```

The sky turns dark and there's thunder and lightning.

Rain falls on Jane.

Spectators on the bleachers raise umbrellas.

Jane is soaked through, as is Conchita.

Jane and Arroyo-Rodriguez retire to the players' lounge while the surface dries out.

Jane and Conchita in shower. They do not speak to one another.

Jane and Conchita drying themselves with towels.

The sky begins to clear.

Spectators take their seats.

Jane and Conchita walk onto court and take positions at their respective baselines.

Jane serves.

Conchita starts to miss everything as Jane moves up a gear and uses her forehand with great effect.

Conchita hits a string of double faults,
balls flying long and netted shots. She loses
the next eight games with Jane leading 6-1,
4-0.

INSET
- - - - - - - - - - - - - -
SCOREBOARD

	Set 1	Set 2
Bennington	6	4
Arroyo-Rodriguez	1	0

- - - - - - - - - - - - - -

Jane slams an ace. She leads 6-1, 5-1.

INSET
- - - - - - - - - - - - - - - - -
SCOREBOARD

	Set 1	Set 2	Set 3
Bennington	6	5	
Arroyo-Rodriguez	1	1	

- - - - - - - - - - - - - - - - -

Conchita claws her way back into the match
as her service rhythm returns. Jane, sensing
victory a little too early, makes a number of
unforced errors. Conchita wins five games in a
row.

INSET
- - - - - - - - - - - - - - -
SCOREBOARD

	Set 1	Set 2
Bennington	6	5
Arroyo-Rodriguez	1	6

- - - - - - - - - - - - - -

Jane serves.

INSET
- - - - - - - - - - - - - - - - -
SCOREBOARD
	Game	Set 1	Set 2
Bennington	30	6	5
Arroyo-Rodriguez	30	1	6
- - - - - - - - - - - - - - - - -

At 30-all, Conchita comes within two points of taking the set, but Jane makes sure that it's as close as she gets.

INSET
- - - - - - - - - - - - - - - - -
SCOREBOARD
	Game	Set 1	Set 2
Bennington	30	6	5
Arroyo-Rodriguez	15	1	6
- - - - - - - - - - - - - - - - -

INSET
- - - - - - - - - - - -
SCOREBOARD
	Game
Bennington	0
Arroyo-Rodriguez	30
- - - - - - - - - - - -

Jane holds serve to force a tie-break and it is as good as over.

INSET
- - - - - - - - - - - - - -
SCOREBOARD

	Set 1	Set 2
Bennington	6	5
Arroyo-Rodriguez	1	6
- - - - - - - - - - - - - -

Jane looks desperate during her opponent's incredible comeback.

Suddenly, she displays the mettle of a champion. She lets loose a string of blazing forehands to take the tie-beak 7-3.

INSET
- - - - - - - - - - - - - -
SCOREBOARD

	Set 1	Set 2
Bennington	6	7
Arroyo-Rodriguez	1	6
- - - - - - - - - - - - - -

Jane and Conchita walk to the net and shake hands. Jane goes to the bench and packs up racquet. The CROWD is applauding. Jane goes over to fans at side of fence and signs autographs and tennis balls. She is smiling.

EXT. HOTEL ARTS—DAY

INT. LOBBY

Lance, Jane and Louise are lounging in the main lobby area, having drinks. Lance is smoking a cigar and has a large glass of brandy in front of him. He is in a light

blazer. Jane is in a sarong covering her
bathing suit. Louise is looking at a map.

> LOUISE
> The weather here is marvelous. Just
> like California. Are you sure you
> don't want to come along? I'm sure
> Roberto won't mind. He's so proud
> of the city, and I'm just dying to
> see that church on the mountain. The
> view is supposed to be spectacular.

> JANE
> No, you go ahead. Practice all this
> morning's tired me out. I'm just
> going to hang out.

> LOUISE
> Lance?

> LANCE
> No, go ahead. We'll see you later.

ROBERTO SERRA in a white Panama suite stands
at the doorway to the lounge. He smiles and
waves to Louise. She gets up and goes to meet
him.

> LOUISE
> Bye, bye. See you later.

Lance summons the WAITRESS and orders another
drink.

> LANCE
> Jane, you should have something.
> Maybe a glass of wine. It'll loosen
> you up a little. Get you in a

relaxed frame of mind. I've been watching and you've been playing a little tight lately. I don't know what's the matter, but maybe it's the pressure.

                    JANE
What're you drinking?

                    LANCE
Rum. The local rum is very good. You can't find it anywhere else in the world.

                    JANE
OK. I'll have that.

                    LANCE
Senorita, dos mas, por favor.

                    JANE
How did you do it, Lance, I mean when you were on the circuit?

                    LANCE
What do you mean?

                    JANE
I mean playing and practicing day after day. No time for anything else. I mean I often think about how things were back at home, and it seems like they were light years away. I mean we're really grateful for what you've done and everything, and, goodness knows Mom's so happy with all of this, but sometimes I just get so lonely.

Lance reaches over and takes her hand.

                JANE (contd.)
    That's a nice ring you have. It's
    new isn't it?

CLOSE UP diamond ring on Lance's hand.

                LANCE
    Oh, it's a little something I
    picked up in Paris. Listen, Jane,
    the important thing to keep in mind
    is to be bigger than all of this.
    The difference between being good
    and being great is commitment and
    dedication. Keeping your eye on the
    ball. I could have been great, but
    these little things, the glamour,
    the nightlife, the endorsements,
    all of those somehow became more
    important than the game. I want to
    see you succeed where I couldn't.
    (pause)
    Let's have another drink. Senorita,
    dos mas, por favor.

The waitress brings two more drinks. She
hands a slip of paper to Jane.

                JANE
    It's a message from Mom. She's going
    out to dinner with Roberto and then
    to a concert. She says to have
    dinner without her and not to stay
    up and wait for her. Oh, boy! Does
    that sound romantic or what?

                    LANCE
     Looks like I'm the chaperon tonight.

He polishes off his drink.

                    LANCE (contd.)
     What's good enough for the goose is
     good enough for the gander. I'll
     tell you what, Jane, let's go out
     for a night on the town. What do you
     say? I know a great club.

                    JANE
     I need to take a shower.

                    LANCE
     Well, go ahead, shower and get
     dressed. I'll meet you back here.

He signals the waitress.

     Senorita, otra, por favor!

INT. HOTEL ROOM—NIGHT

Jane is changing into evening clothes for
the nightclub. She brushes her hair before a
mirror. Her purse is on the dressing table.
She picks it up and from the wallet inside
she looks at a picture of Roger.

EXT./ INT. CLUB EXOTICA—NIGHT

Lance and Jane are sitting at table with
several empty glasses in front of them. A
stripper is dancing in the background. They
are laughing. Jane is wearing a short black
skirt. Lance puts his hand on her knee.

EXT. BARCELONA STREET

Lance has his arm around Jane's waist.

EXT./INT. HOTEL

Lance takes an orchid from a vase and puts it
in Jane's shoulder strap.

INT. HOTEL CORRIDOR—OUTSIDE JANE'S ROOM

They are obviously drunk as they laugh
tipsily while looking for the door key in
Jane's handbag.

                    LANCE
     Let me help you in. We tennis champs
     have to look after one another.

They enter the suite.

                    LANCE
     A nightcap?

                    JANE
     Oh, no I'm so tired, I'm going to
     sleep. I had such a nice time.

He picks Jane up and carries her into the
bedroom where he places her on the bed.

                    LANCE
     I'm right across the hall. I'll just
     take the key. Call me if you need
     anything.

                    JANE
     (sleepily)

OK.

Lance kisses her on the brow and departs.

Jane goes to dresser and takes out a short nightgown. She undresses before the mirror, combs her hair, turns out the light and crawls into bed. She rests her head on the pillow and falls asleep.

CLOSE UP of Jane's face awakening to NOISE in other room.

> JANE
>
> Mom?

She looks at the clock.

CLOCK—3 A.M.

Lance stands in the doorway. He is holding a full glass of whiskey and is drunk. He totters in.

> LANCE
>
> Jane, I couldn't sleep. Let me stay with you.

> JANE
>
> Oh, go back to bed. Mom'll be back soon.

> LANCE
>
> No way. Louise is enjoying the good life. And that's what we should do.

LANCE comes over to the side of the bed.

LANCE
You asked before about how one
handles all of this, the fame, the
celebrity, and the constant on-
the-go. You go with the flow, go with
the flow. I can't tell you how I feel
with all of these vital young bodies
around me all the time. Jane, do an
old man a favor, and let me enjoy a
taste of youth again.

JANE
Lance, I admire you so, but this is
so wrong. You should go back to your
room.

Lance reaches over, grabs her and forces
himself on top of her. Jane struggles as he
slides her nightgown up and forces himself on
her. She starts to scream, but he puts his
hand over her mouth.

LANCE
You owe me, Jane. You owe this old
man.

Jane's leans her head back.

JANE
Sigh . . .

INT. JANE'S HOTEL ROOM—DAY

Jane wakes up blurry-eyed. Louise is in a
chair across the room from Jane's bed having
a cup of coffee and reading a newspaper.

JANE
How was your evening, Mom?

LOUISE
Wonderful, absolutely wonderful.
Roberto's so dignified. We went to
dinner at this marvelous seafood
restaurant on the wharf, and then
the concert. What a magnificent old
concert hall. Then we went for a
long drive into the country in his
sportscar, a Lamborghini. We went
up the coast on a long ride up the
Costa Brava, and then we took a long
walk on the beach. And then some
chorizo and then here we are.

JANE
That sounds nice, Mom.

LOUISE
And what did you guys do?

JANE
Oh, nothing.

LOUISE
Alberto asked us to spend next
summer on his ranch. Isn't that
exciting. Tad, too. It would be
wonderful for all of us to spend a
holiday together.

JANE
Mom . . .

LOUISE
And we could be with Tad . . .

Jane walks into the bathroom and looks at herself in the mirror. There are deep circles under her eyes. She takes a bottle of capsules from the medicine cabinet, fills a glass of water from the tap and swallows them.

EXT. AMERICAN AIRLINES—AIRPLANE IN AIR—DAY

INT. PLANE

Jane is sound asleep wrapped up in blanket in seat. Louise is reading a copy of Vogue magazine.

> PILOT (V.O.)
> We'll be landing at Los Angeles International Airport in a few minutes. Please make sure your seat belts are secure and your seats upright. I certainly hope you enjoyed flying with us today.

EXT. STADIUM—DAY

BANNER—"WOMEN'S TOURNAMENT"

INT. PRESS BOX

> HORNSBY
> A beautiful day here in sunny Southern California for one of the most prestigious tournaments in women's tennis. This year there's a lot to look forward to as a new crop of young players takes the court. We'll be watching new, young hot players like KATRINA LUSHENKO, from

Russia, ANNIE WIDGEN, from England,
CONCHITA ARROYO-RODRIGUEZ from
Spain, and Southern California's own
Jane Bennington, who took the French
open this year and captured the
hearts of French tennis fans.

                    CHRIS
          Yes, it promises to be an exciting
          tournament with so many good new
          young players.

INT. ROGER'S HOUSE—SIMULTANEOUS

Roger and SEVERAL CLASSMATES are gathered
around the television watching the game. They
are drinking sodas and eating popcorn.

INT. STADIUM, COURT

Jane bobs up and down. Sweat is pouring off
her. She is all intense concentration.

NATASHA LUKASHEVA, a slim spitfire with raven
hair and jet black eyes, wipes perspiration
from brow, bounces the ball several times and
serves.

CAMERA PANS behind Jane as she runs for the
ball and serves it back smartly.

Natasha aggressively runs across court and
fires the ball back.

CLOSE UP of Jane's face as she hits ball
back.

Natasha takes the first set as she shoots the ball over Jane's head.

INSET
- - - - - - - - - - -
SCOREBOARD

	Game	Set 1
Bennington	15	4
Lukasheva	40	6
- - - - - - - - - - -

Jane fights back and takes the second easily 6-1.

INSET
- - - - - - - - - - - - - -
SCOREBOARD

	Game	Set 1	Set 2
Bennington	0	4	6
Lukasheva	15	6	1
- - - - - - - - - - - - - -

Jane looks as though she might waltz though the third set as well. Natasha, however, is not to be rolled over and fights all the way to reach five-all in the final set.

INSET
- - - - - - - - - - - - - - - - -
SCOREBOARD

	Game	Set 1	Set 2	Set 3
Bennington	0	4	1	5
Lukasheva	15	6	6	5
- - - - - - - - - - - - - - - - -

Five-all in the third set. Natasha serves.

Natasha has eight points to hold serve, but the game eventually goes Jane's way on her sixth break point when Natasha mis-hits the ball so badly it merely rolls along the ground.

INSET

- - - - - - - - - - - - - - - - - -

SCOREBOARD

	Game	Set 1	Set 2	Set 3
Bennington	0	4	1	6
Lukasheva	15	6	6	5

- - - - - - - - - - - - - - - - - -

The crowd gives a standing ovation at the changeover.

INT. PRESS BOX

> CHRIS
> The game lasted twenty minutes and contained 32 points and thirteen deuces. It's got to be one of, if not the longest singles game in the history of Grand Slam tennis.

> HORNSBY
> Overall, Chris, the final of this tournament turned out to be an epic two-hour, two-minute battle between Bennington and Lukasheva that will go down in history, also, of course, as one of the finest women's matches ever played, although it will be remembered for even just that one game in the third set.

Jane serves out for a 4-6, 6-1, 7-5 win.

INSET
- - - - - - - - - - - - - -
SCOREBOARD
　　　　　Set 1 Set 2 Set 3
Bennington　4　　6　　7
Lukasheva　6　　1　　5
- - - - - - - - - - - - - -

CAMERA FOLLOWS Jane overcome with emotion, as
she runs off court and up through the back
of the stands to embrace Louise and Eddie
and Claudia Schiffer in their seats. On her
return journey to Center Court, she lets out
a chilling scream that expresses not only her
joy at winning, but also her good fortune at
making such an incredible escape.

There's a full crowd in the stands.

INT. PRESS BOX

　　　　　　　　CHRIS
　　If you're just joining us, we're
　　into the semi-final round of this
　　very exciting tournament, one of
　　the best in years. Here's the way
　　it looks on day three. SOLFOOS
　　eliminated KVIST and REID beat
　　ARROYO-RODRIGEUZ in an upset.
　　That means Bennington will play
　　KELLY REID and the winner of that
　　match will play the winner of the
　　NAZDROVIA/SMELTZ match.

　　　　　　　　HORNSBY
　　KELLY REID has really been moving
　　up. The big question here is whether
　　she'll be able to keep up those hard

serves. This will be her fourth
straight game, with little rest.

Kelly waltzes through early rounds. At first
it looks as though Reid's attempt to continue
her onslaught will be halted. She takes the
first set.

INSET
- - - - - - - -
SCOREBOARD

	Set 1
Bennington	1
Reid	6

- - - - - - - -

Kelly is a break ahead at 2-0 in the second.

INSET
- - - - - - - - - - - - - - -
SCOREBOARD

	Game	Set 1	Set 2
Bennington	30	0	0
Reid	0	6	2

- - - - - - - - - - - - - - -

Jane starts to play amazing tennis. She hits
a stream of winners, including several really
sensational key topspin backhands, recovering
from a set and love-two down.

Jane wins in three sets 5-7, 6-2, 6-1.

INSET
- - - - - - - - - - - - - - - - -
SCOREBOARD

	Game	Set 1	Set 2	Set 3
Bennington	40	5	6	6
Reid	0	7	2	1

- - - - - - - - - - - - - - - - -

INSET—TELEVISION SET

                    CHRIS
    What a tournament this has been
    so far. We've arrived at the final
    match here. Get set for some terrific
    tennis going for the championship,
    Jane Bennington and AMANDA SMELTZ of
    Germany.

COURT

Jane is bobbing up and down.

Amanda bounces the ball several times and
serves.

Jane runs for the ball and slams it back.

Amanda runs across court and hits the ball
back.

Jan hits the ball back.

Amanda dashes after ball and slams it back.

Jane runs after the ball. She reaches out and
then collapses on the court.

INT. PRESS BOX

                    CHRIS
Something's happened to Bennington.
She was reaching for the ball
and just seemed to collapse. The
officials are out on the court, and
there's her trainer/manager.

                    HORNSBY
She can't get up. It didn't look as
though she tripped or stumbled on
anything.

                    CHRIS
They've called for a stretcher.

PARAMEDICS put Jane on stretcher and carry
her off the field to the sound of APPLAUSE
from the CROWD.

                    HORNSBY
What an upset! It looks as though
this game is over. Two very well
matched players. But Jane Bennington
is off the course and won't be
returning for this match. We'll
report back from the clubhouse
as soon as we can find out what
happened.

                    CHRIS
Yes, that's it. The officials have
called the game and given it to
Smeltz by default.

INSET

- - - - - - - -

SCOREBOARD

        Match
Bennington   0
Smeltz   1

- - - - - - - -

INT. LOCKER ROOM—DAY

Jane sits on an examining table. Louise and
Lance watch a DOCTOR.

> DOCTOR
> I can't be sure until we take
> some tests at the hospital but it
> looks to me like a case of nervous
> exhaustion.

> LOUISE
> Well she has seemed a little tired
> lately and edgy, I don't know why.

> LANCE
> What about the rest of the
> tournament?

> DOCTOR
> I'm afraid that's out of the
> question. Jane is going to have to
> take a long rest.

INT. HOSPITAL ROOM—DAY

Jane is on the phone with Roger.

> ROGER (V.O.)
> You'll be alright, Jane. Don't
> worry.

> JANE
> I don't care anymore, this was all
> wrong.

> ROGER (V.O.)
> What do you mean?

> JANE
> I can't be what others want me to
> be. I really don't know who I really
> am anymore.

She puts the phone down in its cradle.

INT. LANCE'S APARTMENT

Lance picks up PHONE HANDLE, which is
RINGING.

> LOUISE (V.O.)
> Lance, Jane's disappeared!

> LANCE
> What do you mean?

> LOUISE (V.O.)
> Her suitcase and some of her
> clothing are gone. I don't know
> where she's gone. She didn't leave a
> message.

> LANCE
> Oh, she'll turn up somewhere.

> LOUISE (V.O.)
> You don't sound very concerned.

> LANCE
> After what I put into her career.
> And then to just have it fall apart
> when everything was about to click.
> No. I've been thinking and I'm going
> back to the club as the pro; I've
> made enough, for a while.

EXT. CHICAGO—CITY STREET—DAY

Jane is sitting in doorway of building on a
major thoroughfare. She has a blanket over
her legs. Her hair is scraggly and she is
wearing jeans and a T-shirt. She is taking
sips foam a bottle of red wine. A cup is in
front of her with a few coins in it.

Jane walks through the street at dusk. She
is wearing a jacket. It is cold out, and the
wind is blowing. She stops in front of a
coffee shop and looks in. A businessman at a
table sees her staring in and comes out. He
invites her inside.

Jane is eating a hamburger and fries while
the businessman watches.

EXT. HOTEL—NIGHT

INT. HOTEL ROOM

Businessman throws Jane on the bed and
unbuckles his trousers.

INT. BENNINGTON HOUSE—NIGHT

Louise picks up RINGING PHONE

> SHERRIFF (V.O.)
> Mrs. Bennington, Mrs. Louise
> Bennington?

> LOUISE
> Yes.

> SHERRIFF
> This is Deputy Tim O'Brien of the
> Chicago Sheriff's Department. We
> have some news on the missing
> person's report you filed on your
> daughter.

> LOUISE
> Where did you say you are calling
> from?

> SHERRIFF
> Chicago, ma'am. The juvenile vice
> squad got a tip on a girl fitting
> your daughter's description. We're
> fairly certain it's her because
> the informant said she was wearing
> a little necklace with a tennis
> racquet on it.

> LOUISE
> Oh, my god!

> SHERRIFF
> We can't bring her in without
> a member of the family present
> to authorize it and to make the
> positive identification. Is there any
> chance you could come out here?

                    LOUISE
Oh, my, yes. Yes, of course.
Is she OK?

                    SHERRIFF
Physically, yes, she seems to be.
But she's got herself in with some
pretty rough stuff.

                    LOUISE
Oh, my God. I'll be there just
as soon as I can make plane
reservations. Thank you, deputy.

                    SHERRIFF
Don't mention it, ma'am. Call us
when you know when you'll arrive.

EXT. CHICAGO—STREET CORNER—DAY

Jane is standing on the street corner under
a street light with THREE OTHER PROSTITUTES.
She is wearing a tank top, short tight pink
vinyl shorts and high white boots. The girls
are talking. A car pulls up and a man lowers
the car window. He points to Jane and she
gets in the car with him.

INT. SHERRIFF'S OFFICE—NIGHT

Louise and Roger talk with the Sherriff.

                    SHERRIFF
Now, Mrs. Bennington, this isn't
very pretty. Never is. But your
daughter is disturbed, and in trying
to run away from her problems she's

got herself into a pack more. She's
living with some real street trash
that goes by the name of WILFRED
SMITH over in a fleabag hotel on
fourteenth street. He's got a couple
of other girls living there with
him. He's a pimp, one of those
pimps who take advantage of young
runaways. We've been looking to bust
him and we will one of these days.
Anyway, we need to go over there and
get your daughter.
(to Roger)
Coming along, son? This won't be
pleasant.

                    ROGER
You bet. We've got to get Jane.

EXT. HOTEL—DAY

Police car pulls up in front of dilapidated
residence hotel. Several BLACKS are loitering
in front, smoking and drinking out of a paper
bag. A thin black dog is shuffling trough an
overturned garbage can.

O'Brien, Louise and Roger get out of the
police car. Inside the tiny foyer they look
at the mailboxes and then proceed up the
dimly light narrow stairway until they get to
an apartment door marked "12." The LOUD SOUND
of a television set can be heard through the
door. O'Brien POUNDS on the door. No answer.
He POUNDS again.

                    O'BRIEN
     Open up in there. Sheriff's
     department.

Silence.

                    O'BRIEN
     OK. Here we go.

He kicks the door open.

INT. APARTMENT—DAY

Jane and Wilfred are sitting in the dimly lit
dingy room on a half-collapsed couch. Light
filters through sheets that have been thrown
up as curtains across the window. They are
watching TV. On the table in front of them
are bottles of beer, an ashtray, an empty
pizza box, cigarette packs and other debris.
Jane is in a short flimsy negligee open at
the front showing her bare breasts and bikini
panties. Wilfred, a thin black man, is
wearing boxer underwear, a sleeveless T-shirt
and a black bandana wrapped around his head.
A large gold chain and medallion hang from
his neck. He leaps to his feet as door BURSTS
open and the three enter.

                   WILFRED
     Hey! What the fuck, man! Who give
     you the right to step into a man's
     castle? Get the fuck out, man!

                   O'BRIEN
     Cook County Sheriff's Department,
     you lowlife. If I were you, I'd just
     sit there and shut up.

                      113

(Pause)
Mrs. Bennington, is this your
daughter?

                    LOUISE
Yes.

                    JANE
Mom, Roger. What are you doing here?

                    O'BRIEN
Get dressed, Miss Bennington. You're
going home.

                    JANE
No, I want to stay here.

                    WILFRED
Yeah, man, you fuck. You see she
want to be here with her man. You
asshole.

                    O'BRIEN
One more word out of you, I told
you, and I'll put you away so you
never see the light of day.

Louise has placed her coat over Jane and she
leads her out the door.

Wilfred jumps to his feet.

                    WILFRED
Hey, Jane, you don't have to do what
that ol' bitch say. You are a free
woman.

O'Brien blocks Wilfred as Jane and Louise
exit.

                    O'BRIEN
     I warned you, you piece of shit.

O'Brien drives a hard right into his stomach.
He doubles over. O'Brien brings up his knee
hard into his groin and he sinks to the floor.

                    O'BRIEN
     Let's get out of here, son.

O'Brien opens the door and walks out. Roger,
who is behind him, turns and kicks the
prostate body in the stomach before following
him out the door.

EXT. CALIFORNIA—ROCKY ROAD SANITORIUM—DAY

SUPER—"SIX MONTHS LATER"

Jane and Roger are sitting on the lawn under
a tree. It is a bright clear sunny day. Off
in distance a brown and white cocker spaniel
PUPPY breaks from a MAN and WOMAN visiting
with an ELDERLY WOMAN in a wheel chair. The
puppy runs over to Jane and Roger.

                    JANE
     I just gave up on myself, it was
     too much. Studying all the time,
     practicing, playing, traveling,
     wanting to win, not wanting to let
     anybody down, especially Dad — and
     Mom, too, of course—and I just had
     to escape.

                    ROGER
I never lost faith in you, Jane.

                    JANE
Oh, Roger, you're so sweet. What
would I ever do without you?

                    ROGER
Well, Jane, now what?

                    JANE
Oh, I don't know. Go back to school,
I guess. The doctor says I'm well
enough to leave. I think Mrs.
Moffett was right all along. I can
still go to college.

                    ROGER
And become a veterinarian.

                    JANE
And become a veterinarian. No more
tennis. My only real regret is that
I've let Dad down. He'd have been so
proud of me, and he definitely wasn't
a quitter.

                    ROGER
But, Jane, you don't have to quit.
You don't have to give up one for
the other. Maybe you just don't have
to be tennis pro. Maybe you just
have to like to play tennis. Play
it.

                    ROGER
Well, and be the best veterinarian
in the world.

EXT. PUBLIC TENNIS COURTS—DAY

Roger is lobbing tennis balls to Jane who is
smashing them back over the net.

Roger rallies with Jane.

Roger sits on a bench watching Jane play a
very vigorous match with another GIRL.

Jane and Roger walking along side the tennis
courts with flowering trees in the background.

> JANE
> I don't know when I've ever been so
> happy. I mean really happy.

> ROGER
> Jane, I love you. After college,
> let's get married. You can have your
> veterinarian practice. We'll buy a
> big old farmhouse with plenty of
> animals. We'll raise a family.

> JANE
> Oh, Roger!

INT. BENNINGTON HOUSE—DAY

Jane and Louise are in the living room. Jane
is pouring over college course catalogs.

> JANE
> Tufts offers a four-year degree in
> medicine. And then you can go on to
> vet school.

                    LOUISE
        Tufts is awfully expensive, dear,
        and then there's living expenses
        and all of that while away from
        home. Maybe one of the local state
        colleges would be better.

                     JANE
        When did expense ever enter the
        picture? We made so much money from
        the tournaments. We're well off. We
        can afford whatever we want. Can't
        we?

                    LOUISE
        Well, Jane, there's something I've
        been meaning to tell you. We really
        don't have much money at all.
        Lance saw to that. Between making
        contracts to his own advantage and
        a lot of bad investments with that
        shyster accountant of his, we've got
        very little left. I'm sorry, dear.
        But I'm afraid we'll have to find a
        scholarship for you. And I guess
        they'll have me back at the Seven-
        Eleven. Oh God, newspapers, coffee,
        donuts and cigarettes.

Fingers gold necklace.

                 LOUISE (contd.)
        I should have married Roberto when
        he asked me, even though he was
        twice my age.

INT. LAGUNA HILLS HIGH SCHOOL—DAY

                     118

CORRIDOR

CLASS BELL RINGS and students pour into the
hallway. Roger spots Jane and comes running
up to her.

                    ROGER
     I was just talking with Denise and
     she told me there's a big charity
     benefit tournament coming up over at
     Marbella. It's a one-time tournament
     and the Mercedes-Benz Dealers of
     California sponsor it.

                    JANE
     So?

                    ROGER
     So, the grand prize is fifty thousand
     dollars cash.

                    JANE
     But Roger, you know professional
     tennis is over for me. I can't go
     through that again. You know that.

                    ROGER
     You don't have to go back on the
     tournament circuit. This would be
     the chance to make back all the
     money Lance skimmed and wasted by
     your mother. To afford college. So
     we can get married. To pursue our
     dreams, our life together.

                    JANE
     I don't know if I can play any more,
     if I'm any good any more.

> ROGER
> Of course you are. You're just as
> good as you ever were. Winning this
> tournament will prove to you and
> everyone else you care about that
> you've recovered and give us the
> money for a fresh start on life.
> I'll ask Coach Vincent at school to
> work with you as your coach for the
> tournament. I know he'll do it. He's
> always been so proud of you.

> JANE
> Well, OK. But just this once. You
> were right. I don't want to be the
> best tennis pro in the world. I just
> want to be the best veterinarian.

EXT. MARBELLA COUNTRY CLUB—DAY

BANNER—"SOUTHERN CALIFORNIA MERCEDES BENZ
DEALERS WOMEN'S OPEN FOR THE BENEFIT OF THE
ALZHEIMER'S DISEASE ASSOCIATION"

There is a full crowd in the stands.

Veronica and Lance pull up in bright red
sports car. A very sleek, tanned Veronica
gets out. She is wearing a short classic
traditional white tennis skirt and polo
shirt. They pass by Jane on their way into
the club.

> VERONICA
> So, our little star has fallen back
> to earth.

INT. PRESS BOX

                    CHRIS
Hi. Welcome to Mission Viejo,
California, a nationally ranked
tournament for a good cause. We'll
be seeing some new faces and some
familiar faces. One of those is Jane
Bennington, who's been off the tour
for a year now after a stunning
career collapse.

                    HORNSBY
We understand she's been training
with her old high school coach, Ned
Vincent. So many good young players
have come out of California school
tennis. Bennington's pro coach has
been working with Veronica, a real
comer.

                    CHRIS
Just one of the stories we'll be
watching unfold here today.

COURT

Jane is bobbing up and down. Sweat is pouring
off her. She is tense.

                              FADE TO:

MELANIE MORROW, a slim, trim, perky teenager,
wipes perspiration from brow, bounces the
ball several times and serves.

Jane runs for the ball and serves it back
smartly.

Jane takes advantage of a seemingly
distracted Melanie to roll through the
first set. Melanie argues calls and,
clearly unhappy with the outcomes, becomes
increasingly flustered.

INSET

- - - - - - - -
               Set 1
Bennington   6
Morrow   1
- - - - - - - -

Jane punishes Melanie's mediocre second serve
and holds on when Melanie rallies from a 4-2
deficit in the second set.
Melanie has two chances to even the match in
the second set, breaking Jane's serve to go
up 5-4 and 6-5, but each time Melanie breaks
back and the set goes to a tiebreaker.

INSET

- - - - - - - - - - - -
               Set 1 Set 2
Bennington   6   6
Morrow   1   2
- - - - - - - - - - - -

In the tiebreaker, Jane gets to match point
by approaching off a deep forehand and
tapping a backhand volley. Then she wins
with a 108mph first serve that kicks wide of
Melanie's forehand in the deuce court and
forces the lunging Melanie to return wide and
long, a stunning and winning match serve.

INSET

- - - - - - - - - - -
	Set 1	Set 2
Bennington	6	7
Morrow	3	6

- - - - - - - - - - -

INT. PRESS BOX

                    CHRIS
     Showdown time here at Mission
     Viejo, California. The final round,
     which promises to be a doozy: Jane
     Bennington against Veronica Tyson.
     Bennington's fought her way through
     several tough opponents—Reid and
     Schwartz—to end up in the final round
     in her first comeback since that
     fateful fall last year.

                    HORNSBY
     The fans are going crazy over
     these two local California girls.
     I know a lot are pulling for Jane
     Bennington but she's got a tough
     row to hoe here. To top it off,
     Veronica is coached by Lance Drake,
     who took Jane to the French open
     and has produced very tough, young
     competitive tennis players.

                    CHRIS
     Well, here we are at center court.
     Let's take a look.

BLEACHERS

Where there is a full crowd.

INT. CORRIDOR LEADING FROM DRESSING ROOMS TO COURT

Lance is waiting at the end of the corridor as Jane heads toward the open light at the end to get onto the court. Lance steps forward and bocks her way.

                    JANE
        Get out of my way. I never want to
        see you again. Ever!

                    LANCE
        I just thought I'd wish my little
        Janie luck before she got onto the
        court. A lot of money to be made out
        there today. Enough for some booze
        and some pills, huh? And maybe a
        little roll in the hay. Remember
        Barcelona?

                    JANE
                (visibly shaken)
        Just get out of my way and leave me
        alone.

                    LANCE
        Yeah, Janie, you were the best piece
        of ass I ever had. I swear. I really
        do.

Jane exits the corridor opening into the sunlight. The CAMERA is ANGLED up toward her face with the CROWD the stands and the sky behind her. She is crying; tears are running down her face.

Jane has her head down. She bounces the ball several times.

She looks up and sees Veronica bobbing up and down. Jane serves.

The ball hits the net.

She serves again and it hits the net. A double fault.

INSET
- - - - - - - - - - - - - - -
SCOREBOARD

	Game	Set 1	Set 2
Bennington	0	0	3
Tyson	15	6	4

- - - - - - - - - - - - - - -

VERONICA wipes perspiration from brow and bounces the ball several times.

CLOSE UP—JANE

She looks into stands.

CLOSE UP—LANCE

He gives her a lascivious smile, runs his tongue over his lips and nods his head up and down.

Veronica serves.

Jane runs for the ball and hits it back smartly.

VERONICA runs across court and hits ball back.

CLOSE UP—

Jane's face as she hits ball back.

Jane feeds Veronica many drop shots and forces many rallies that demand the tireless repetition of a metronome. They take their toll. Jane manages to take the second set.

INSET
- - - - - - - - - - - - - - -
SCOREBOARD

	Game	Set 1	Set 2
Bennington	30	0	6
Tyson	0	6	4

- - - - - - - - - - - - - - -

Late into the third set. Veronica is confident and smug.

Lance gives Veronica a thumbs up.

A long rally ensues.

Veronica takes her eyes from the ball to look at the stands where Lance is.

She buries a swinging forehand volley into the net.

INSET
- - - - - - - - - - - - - - - - - -
SCOREBOARD

	Game	Set 1	Set 2	Set 3
Bennington	30	0	6	6
Tyson	0	6	3	6

- - - - - - - - - - - - - - - - - -

Jane serves for match. She bounces the ball, carefully, six times, three bounces more than he usual.

CLOSE UP of Jane's face as she looks up at the ball in the air in front of her, arches her racquet high and whips it down.

Veronica dashes after the ball across the court, but it sizzles past her at lighting speed and hits just within the corner baseline.

INSET
- - - - - - - - - - - - - - - - - - - -
SCOREBOARD

	Game	Set 1	Set 2	Set 3	
Bennington	40	0	3	6	(7)
Tyson	0	6	6	6	(5)

- - - - - - - - - - - - - - - - - - - -

CENTER COURT

Jane walks to the net to shake hands. Veronica stalks off. CAMERA follows as Jane goes to bench and packs up her racquet. The CROWD is applauding.

Jane goes over to fans at side of fence and signs autographs and tennis balls, happy and smiling.

Veronica slaps Lance and stalks off.

INT. PRESS BOX

> CHRIS
> What a game! Jane Bennington has made as amazing a comeback as any we've ever seen.

> HORNSBY
> Listen to that applause. The fans are certainly delighted.

COURT

Jane is surrounded by Roger, Louise, Tad and the grey-haired Coach Vincent. The TOURNAMENT OFFICIAL hands Jane a check, which she hands over to Roger. He then presents her with the big silver tournament trophy. Jane is ecstatically happy. The CAMERA PULLS back to an overview of the court, as the MUSIC comes up.

Three Air Force fighter jets trail smoke, splitting off into a triad.

> FADE OUT:

> END

Author's Biography

Jack Sholl is a former journalist and national
editor with The Associated Press In New York
and has worked on newspapers in New Jersey,
Pennsylvania and Virginia. He is the author of
a number of screenplays. He lives in Florida.

Editorial assistant: Veronica Rodriguez